The Axe Was About to Fall

Longarm whirled, his Colt in his fist without conscious thought. Beside him Goose Coe was almost as quick. Both men crouched at the ready with revolvers in their hands.

It was that big son of a bitch from the night before. Dave, they had called him.

He had to be sober by now. The bartender had said he was mean when he was dry, and he was sure as hell coming on mean right now.

His face was flushed dark red with fury, and he was breathing heavily. There was an ugly look of grim determination on him, and he ran silently toward Longarm with a double-bitted axe upraised and ready to strike.

There was no question at all that he intended to use it. If Longarm and Coe had not heard him coming he could have—and Longarm genuinely believed would have—split Longarm's skull apart like a ripe apple under the filed blade of that gleaming axe head.

Longarm fired.

The Colt bellowed and bucked in his hand, and a damp red spot appeared on Dave's chest. The big man stumbled but kept coming...

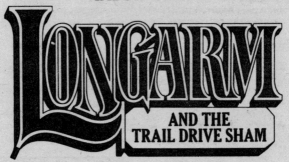

TABOR EVANS

LONGARM

AND THE
TRAIL DRIVE SHAM

J(R)

A JOVE BOOK

LONGARM AND THE TRAIL DRIVE SHAM

A Jove Book/published by arrangement with
the author

PRINTING HISTORY
Jove edition/February 1987

ISBN: 0-515-08883-8

Jove Books are published by The Berkley Publishing Group,
200 Madison Avenue, New York, NY 10016.
The words "A JOVE BOOK" and the "J" with sunburst
are trademarks belonging to Jove Publications, Inc.

Chapter 1

Longarm came into the office whistling and grinning and ready for anything—or nearly anything. After spending the last sixteen hours saying non-stop goodbyes to Margaret Bassington, there were a few things he might not be ready for. But anything else he could handle. He felt just plain good this morning.

"*Good* morning, Henry." Longarm removed his flat-crowned brown Stetson and sailed it across the room toward the hatrack. The spinning Stetson fluttered past the prongs of the rack and the brim thumped loudly into the wall, but even that did not put a damper on Deputy Long's good humor. He left the hay lying where it fell and reached for a cheroot.

Henry, U.S. Marshal Billy Vail's chief clerk, gave Longarm an odd look. Henry was *always* giving Custis Long odd looks, or so it sometimes seemed. Longarm sometimes thought that old Henry was a bit of a prig. Still, he was steady. Vail and his deputies could count on Henry when the chips were down, and that meant something. Certainly there was no animosity between them. Longarm and Henry were simply . . . different.

"Cat got your tongue, Henry?" Longarm asked. He was still feeling chipper. He perched on the edge of Henry's already cluttered desk and grinned down at the bespectacled man.

Even with Longarm seated, Henry had to look up a considerable distance to see him. Longarm was something over six feet tall, with the whipcord build of a natural horseman.

"What's that you're working on, Henry?" Longarm snatched up the topmost paper from a pile in front of the clerk and pretended to scrutinize it. He was determined to get some kind of rise out of the prissy fellow.

The slip was an expense voucher, part of the flood of paperwork that kept poor Henry occupied every day and many nights. Longarm winked at Henry and looked back toward the voucher sheet, prepared to read the thing out loud if necessary.

It wasn't necessary. Henry lunged out of his chair and snatched the voucher out of Longarm's grip, yelping in protest. The expense voucher, Longarm saw before the sheet disappeared from under his nose, was Billy Vail's own. He thought it a pity that he had not had time to really read the thing. It might have given him something to twist Billy's tail with on this bright and beautiful Monday morning.

"Now, now, Henry. No need to get yourself exercised. So what've you got for me today? Warrants? Subpoenas? Nursemaid for some visiting bigwig? I'm ready for anything today, Henry." Longarm grinned again.

Henry did not return the grin. In fact, Henry was not looking him in the eye, Longarm realized.

And those odd looks Henry had been giving him . . . they might not have been exactly the usual sort of smug

2

disapproval. In fact, now that Longarm was paying attention, Henry seemed a bit hangdog this morning.

Longarm looked down at him with a broader grin than ever. "A little too much of the grape last night, Henry?"

Longarm's good humor was not infectious. Henry gave him a troubled look and motioned toward the door to Billy Vail's private office. "He wants to see you. First thing." Henry looked quickly down again. The marshal's personal, and presumably private, expense voucher had been quickly shuffled underneath a pile of other papers, Longarm noticed.

"Okay," Longarm said cheerfully. "Whatever the boss wants, I shall provide." He would have winked at Henry again, but Henry was not looking. Longarm shrugged, hopped off Henry's desk, and wandered into Vail's office without knocking.

Billy Vail, chief marshal for the Denver District, United States Justice Department, was seated behind his desk. Normally pink-cheeked and robust, if a trifle plump, Vail looked positively haggard this morning, as though he had not gotten much sleep lately. His necktie was loose and the wings of his stiff collar were flying at odd angles. He had not shaved this morning. Even his hair, the pale fringe of it that he had left, was rumpled.

"Damn, Billy, you look like you've been on the same bender that has ol' Henry so out of shape this morning."

Billy Vail looked up at him and scowled, but he didn't snarl or curse or even rebuke the tall deputy. Longarm decided that there might be some serious business afoot here. He put his wisecracks aside for the time being and quietly took a seat in front of Billy's desk.

Without so much as a word of greeting, Vail pulled a thick folder from the corner of his desk and spread it open before him. He rummaged through the contents for several silent minutes before he closed the file again, turned it around, and shoved it over toward Longarm.

Even before he opened the thing Longarm was surprised, mostly by the sheer volume of it.

The usual case file, at least at the beginning of an investigation, was seldom more than a page or two of material: a warrant, a writ, a telegraph message form, sometimes no more than a pencil scrawl on a scrap of paper where someone had jotted down an informant's suspicions.

This folder must have held two score sheets of paper, most of them copies of wires sent and received, requests for information and responses from as near as Ogallala, Nebraska and as far away as Brownsville, Texas, which was just about as far south as you could get without leaving the United States. Then Longarm corrected himself on that point. The telegrams came from even farther away than that. There was one from the Mexican authorities at Nuevo Laredo too. Or was that farther north than Brownsville? Longarm could not remember. And right now, after seeing the look on Billy Vail's face, Long did not want to ask him about it, even though Billy used to work that area as a field man himself, before someone had the great good sense to give the political appointment of a marshal's job to someone—in this case Vail—who was actually competent to do the job.

Longarm grunted and continued to read.

Later, when he went back out to Henry's desk, he closed Vail's door carefully behind him. Longarm looked just as serious now as Henry did.

This time Henry's eyes lifted to meet Longarm's.

"This is awful thin, Henry," Longarm said in a low voice.

Henry's expression changed from nervous to stubborn. "There is sufficient jurisdiction. . . ."

"Yeah, I know. He told me," Longarm replied. "My question is, will the U. S. Attorney agree." Longarm shook his head. "Awful thin," he repeated.

"Did you . . . ?" Henry seemed unwilling to finish the question.

"What kind of ingrate do you take me for?" Longarm

4

snapped at him. "Of course I took the case."

Henry gave him a wan smile. "If nothing else," he said, "we can all have company, then, when we go to apply for new jobs." His smile firmed, seemed more genuine now.

Longarm smiled back at him. The expression turned into a grin. Soon both men were chuckling and then laughing out loud.

"I'll see you later, Henry. I got to change out of these city clothes and get on the road."

Longarm stood in front of the mirror over the bureau in his rented room, checking to see that he had the effect he wanted. He grunted softly to himself. Half of the sound was amusement at what he saw in that mirror, but the other half was consternation.

A few different turns, not all that many years ago, a few more bottles, some slightly different judgments made, and he could easily have become the man who stared back at him out of the mirror.

Still much the same on the outside, of course. Still tall and lean and brown and muscled, with that sweep of rich brown moustache and a go-to-hell look in the pale eyes. But there was a difference.

The man in the mirror was ... seedy. The borrowed jeans were saddle-worn and a touch too long, draping themselves over the chap-hooks on the borrowed Mexican spurs. The secondhand boots with fancy, Texas-style stitching were run over at the heels and long unpolished. He wore no vest, just a cloth coat with patches at the elbows. Suspenders instead of a belt at the waist. Even the old, comfortable Stetson had been set aside in favor of a drab and dusty Kossuth with a brim that flopped low to hood his eyes. The most prominent thing about him now was the familiar Colt that rode his belly just to the left of the gunbelt buckle. That he would not discard.

Seedy, he confirmed. That was exactly what was needed here. For a moment he thought about letting himself go unshaven for a time. But that might be a bit too much. Better, he decided, to remain shaved but let the normally groomed moustache straggle instead. It would lend just a touch more to the impression without arousing suspicions.

Longarm grunted again, this time with satisfaction.

He picked up his saddlebags. The carpetbag would remain at the bottom of his wardrobe this time, and he would be carrying no telegraph key or other normal implements of the trade. He lifted the borrowed stock saddle with a much-used hemp catch rope and rifle scabbard attached. The McClellan he usually rode would have to be left behind also.

Ready, Longarm went out to the street where a hansom waited for him. He did not expect to be riding in hired style for a while again. Not after he got to Dodge. It was not the sort of thing a saddlebum would want to do. Not even a saddlebum who was flush with money from unexplained sources.

Longarm's lips tightened into something that might have been taken for a smile, and the driver turned the rig toward the railroad depot.

He left the train at Larned, tired and smelling of cigar smoke and coal cinders from the long hours of boredom and the discomfort of even the most plush seating provided by the passenger cars.

Denver to Julesburg to Omaha to Kansas City and finally back west again to Larned was the long way around, but it was the quickest route to Dodge City, at least until the steadily expanding rail lines moved west.

Longarm stretched his aching muscles and picked up the heavy stock saddle that was temporarily replacing his own light McClellan. The stock saddle would be a comfortable thing to ride day in and day out, but it was hard on a horse's back. The difference was that a cowhand could choose to use, and normally did use, three different horses during his day and night of labors, but a cavalry trooper on patrol was stuck with a single mount for the course of a full campaign. Besides, the army cared more about its horses than about its troopers; the horses were more expensive to acquire and maintain.

Off in the distance Longarm could see the big garrison flag over Fort Larned. The fort was the object of his stop-over here, but he did not want to display any open interest in it. He settled instead for a second-rate hotel close to the railroad station, found a youngster who for twenty-five cents was delighted to deliver a note for him, and then hunted up a first-rate restaurant. The food on the trains had been as revolting to the taste as it had been expensive.

"Steak," Longarm ordered, ignoring the menu a waiter tried to offer, "tallow fried till it hollers quit. Taters fried along with it. Beans if you got them."

The waiter offered a sour face but made no open comment. He tucked the menu back under his arm and disappeared in the direction of the kitchen. At the other tables nearby, the better class of Larned residents and more prosperous travelers were dining on roast chicken or passenger pigeon and dumplings. Longarm had ordered the trailhand's standby. It did not hurt that he happened to like the simple meal of beef and potatoes.

Coffee was brought immediately, complete with refills already available in a small silver pot resting on a saucer. Thoughtful, Longarm thought. Aloud he made a pretended fuss over finding more coffee in the little pot. Not that anyone was apt to be paying attention to him at this point, but it never hurt to be careful. He wouldn't want anyone raising awkward questions about a rough-looking cowboy's table manners.

"If you need anything else, sir . . ."

"Naw, but if I do I'll let out a war whoop."

"Yes," the waiter said primly. "I am sure you will, sir." The man's face was a mask, blank and closed, as he turned to his other duties. Longarm very nearly betrayed himself with a grin of wry amusement.

7

Longarm took a swallow of the coffee—slightly weak by campfire standards—lighted a cheroot and leaned back expansively in his chair. He kicked the other chair at his table out to the side and propped his boots on its embroidered seat. He had to be careful of the over-large Mexican spurs he was wearing. The things were much more awkward than his normal military-style spurs, and he had to watch where the damn things were planted or risk tangling them.

The businessmen at the table next to his seemed to be ignoring him. An elderly woman in a family group at another nearby table frowned when Longarm lighted his cigar, but he ignored her. Across the room there was a most attractive woman dining alone. He wasn't sure, but he thought her eyes—blue? green? it was hard to tell at the distance—kept cutting his way. Longarm decided that it would be completely in character for him to admire the filly's conformation, so he spent the rest of his time while waiting for the meal by ogling her while he smoked.

Later, while he was finishing a slab of fresh apple pie and the last of the coffee, the woman was approached by a dandy in spats and bowler.

"No!" she said sharply, and much more loudly than was necessary in the quiet, polite atmosphere of the restaurant. This time he was quite sure that the woman looked directly at him before she turned back to the gentleman who was bending over her table.

Longarm shoved himself away from the table and crossed the room with long, lanky strides. His spur rowels chimed lightly as he moved, and he hooked his thumbs behind his gunbelt and adopted a deliberately arrogant look.

"You got troubles here, ma'am?" he drawled.

Her eyes were definitely green under ringlets of blonde hair. She looked from Longarm to the dandy and back again. "Yes," she said.

Longarm stared down at the much shorter gentleman.

8

His expression might have been carved from a block of ice. "Is that right, mister?" he demanded.

The dandy looked like he wanted to curl up and shrink inside himself. He licked nervously at suddenly dry lips. "Uh, no. No trouble. No, indeed." Considerably paler than he had been a few moments before, the man turned and made a hurried exit from the restaurant.

"How gallant of you, sir." The woman pronounced "gallant" oddly, stressing the second syllable instead of the first. She looked Longarm over as boldly as would a man assessing the points of a bull. He knew what she was seeing. He looked like trouble on the hoof. She seemed to like that. "Would you care to join me?" She smiled. "Sir?"

"Yeah, why not." He pulled out the chair opposite her and plunked down onto it. The other diners seemed to be trying to ignore the two. Longarm thought they were not doing very well at it, but at least they were trying.

The woman introduced herself as Mae Foster. She spelled her first name for him so he would not confuse it with the more common May.

"Custis," Longarm said. "Tom Custis. They call me Long Tom."

"Because you are so tall, Mr. Custis?"

"No," he said bluntly. "There's a better reason than that."

Mae Foster laughed, and the interest in her eyes quickened. Beneath the floor-length drape of the tablecloth he could feel her shoe probe forward, finding his boots and rubbing between them. If the table had been any smaller he expected he might have felt some franker kind of probing as well. Mae Foster apparently liked dangerous men.

"Would you be so kind, sir, as to walk me to my hotel?"

She was staying at a hotel. So she was not a local. That would explain something of her willingness to be so bold in public. And it might explain the poor dandy's approach to her as well. Probably the poor son of a bitch had gotten a come-on from her on the afternoon train. Longarm had

9

not noticed either of them on board, but then he had spent the entire leg of the journey in the smoker, where Mae Foster would not have made an appearance. Now it looked like sweet Mae had found more interesting game to put on her trophy wall. Longarm's good fortune, the other fellow's bad.

"I reckon," he drawled.

"How very kind of you, Long Tom Custis," she said sweetly.

The woman rose. So did Longarm. He neglected to help her with her chair or to offer to pay her bill. Those gestures would only have confused her anyway.

As they left the restaurant Longarm glanced at a Seth Thomas clock mounted on the back wall of the place. It was only a little after seven, and he was not supposed to meet Bradley until ten or later.

He had plenty of time to be polite to Mae Foster before then.

"This way," he said, turning toward the crude accommodations he had taken down near the depot. He suspected that they would enthuse Mae Foster much more than her own undoubtedly elegant room.

He was right.

Chapter 2

The army post was for the most part asleep and silent. Dim lamplight showed only at a very few windows. The sutler's had long since been shuttered and padlocked, and even the most determined drunks seemed to have given up hopes for amusement and gone off to bed. Life at an infantry garrison was not exactly filled with glory and bravura, Longarm knew.

The only movement Longarm could see was that of a yawning sentry, posted on the parade ground for form rather than function, who trudged back and forth in a most un-military manner. Longarm suspected he could have driven a herd of longhorns across the broad, open area without arousing any curiosity from the man. Not that he had any desire to prove the point. He kept to the shadows, past the hospital and then the row of married officers' quarters, and finally came to the adjutant's residence.

Longarm went around to the back of the stone house and tapped softly on the kitchen door.

There was no light inside, but the door was quickly opened. "Yes?" It was a woman's voice, delivered in a whisper.

"Martha?"

"Custis?"

Bradley's wife stepped forward into the starlight long enough to give Longarm a quick hug of warm welcome, then pulled him inside her kitchen. "You're late," she chided.

"Took me longer to walk out here than I expected," Longarm said. There were other reasons too, but he did not want to go into all that.

Martha Bradley shut the door behind him and lighted a candle while her husband wrung Longarm's hand in an extended shake. The graying major seemed genuinely pleased to see this late-night visitor. Despite the late hour, Bradley was in full uniform. Mrs. Bradley had her hair down and was wearing a heavy robe, obviously ready to retire if the men wanted privacy.

"I've been keeping tea and scones hot for you, Custis," Martha said. She checked to make sure the fluffy curtains over the kitchen window were pulled tight together.

"You're as thoughtful as you always were," Longarm said. "And getting prettier every day." Longarm grinned at her husband and shook the older man by the shoulder.

Mrs. Bradley blushed, even though she recognized the untruth of the statement. Surface untruth, anyway. Martha Bradley was one of those rare women who were homely only on the surface. She had an inner something—Longarm had never quite been able to define it—that made her unappealing only at first meeting. The more he came to know her after that, though, the prettier she seemed. At this point Longarm was prepared to argue in all sincerity that Martha Bradley was a truly beautiful woman.

"You're a lucky man, Tom."

12

"Aye, and don't I know it."

Martha set out a cozy-covered teapot and a plate of warm scones and quietly withdrew from the kitchen. If this had been a social call it would not be taking place at this time of night.

"What can I do for you, Custis?" Bradley fumbled for a pipe and tobacco in the pockets of his high-collared uniform blouse.

"You can accept my apologies for keeping you up," Longarm said. "And I have a favor to ask."

Bradley lighted his pipe and shook the match out. "Anything you could ask would be our pleasure to provide, Custis. After what you've done for Martha and me."

Longarm felt slightly uncomfortable with the reminder. That had all been a very long time ago and was not worth remembering, at least the way he saw it. "I need a horse, Tom. And a bill of sale made out to me under a different name. I can't take a remount the way I normally would. They're all branded as government property, and I can't have that this time out."

Bradley smiled. "And here I just thought you were going to seed." The pipe rattled wetly when he drew on it. "The horse and bill of sale are no problem. I have two of my own in the stable. You can have your pick of them. One I brought from back home, so it has never been branded. The other carries an old brand from someplace down south."

"That's the one I'd like then, Tom."

"Done."

"And it wouldn't hurt if you could find some reason to send a wire to the post commander at Fort Dodge."

"Yes?"

Longarm grinned at him. "Kind of warning him to keep an eye on a suspicious character thought to be heading his way."

"You want to be arrested?"

"No, that wouldn't do. Not a warrant, just a warning.

Unspecified suspicions. That sort of thing. Would that be a logical thing for you to do?"

Bradley drew on his pipe for a moment while he thought. "Not on its own. But it is the sort of courtesy I might reasonably tack onto the end of an official communiqué. We're expecting a troop strength report from Dodge in the next day or two. I could add your warning when I acknowledge that."

"That would do," Longarm said.

"Description of this nefarious person?"

Longarm grinned again. "You're looking at him."

Bradley chuckled. "Going out amongst the heathen, are you?"

"Something like that," Longarm agreed.

"Then I shall wish you well. Although Martha and I were hoping you could spend a few days with us. We get to see you so seldom, it seems."

"When this is over, Tom, I just might have a whole lot of free time on my hands. If I do I'll certainly spend some of it with you."

"From the way you say that, Custis, I rather hope you don't. But you know you are welcome here under any circumstances."

"Thanks." Longarm hoped he would not have that kind of free time either. But if Billy Vail was going to the wall with this thing, well, Custis Long would take the trip with him. And the hell with how an office-bound U.S. Attorney might pick it apart afterward. Loyalties, after all, go deeper than paychecks.

Bradley laid his pipe aside and went to get paper and ink to make out the bill of sale for the horse.

"I don't know when I'll be able to get him back to you."

"No matter. If you need him he's yours. If you can't return him at all, no matter." Major Bradley bent over the sheet of paper with a grim look. He was very obviously a man more at home with a saber than a pen. "What name shall I make this out to, Custis?"

"Thomas Custis, also known as Long Tom Custis."

"Isn't that a bit too close to the truth?"

"Just the opposite, I hope. I'm too damn well known in Dodge City, Tom. Been there too many times before. This way if anybody speaks to me when the wrong parties are listening, well, I'll at least have a chance to lie my way out of it."

Bradley grunted and went back to his writing. "I must say," he said when the simple chore was done, "that I am glad I am surrounded by the peace and serenity of army life instead of your dangerous pursuits."

He said it with a straight face, and Longarm had to laugh. Tom Bradley would retire as a mere major, but the man had twice been breveted to higher rank during the recent unpleasantness for extreme gallantry in the face of enemy fire. Peace and serenity indeed! Bradley blew the ink dry and handed the sheet to Longarm.

"You're a gentleman and a scholar, Tom Bradley, and I thank you most kindly."

"Aye, I am," Bradley agreed cheerfully, "so stated by act of Congress, no less." He grinned.

"I should leave now and let you and your bride get some sleep." Longarm started to rise.

Bradley clamped a firm hand on his wrist. "You'll not be running off that easily, 'Long Tom' Custis Long. If I let you get away from here without tea and scones, that bride of mine will flay me alive. And after twenty-two years of blissful marriage, it would not be a fitting end, Custis."

Longarm grinned at his friend and settled back onto the chair. He helped himself to one of the now cool but still flaky and delicious scones.

It was past noon when Longarm rode into Dodge. It had taken him a slow and easy day and a half to make the trip down from Larned. He could have made it in one hard day, but there had been no need for that. He was not in a race. It would take a little time for Tom Bradley's promised wire to

15

reach the fort east of town, and more time for its contents to be circulated. Besides, the men whose acquaintance he intended to make here had probably not arrived themselves.

Dodge had changed little since the last time Longarm saw it. At this time of year it was still surrounded by herds of long-legged, long-horned cattle that would have left Texas months earlier and had arrived to await sale and shipment to the packing plants in Kansas City or even on to points east. Longarm had been weaving his way between herds of placidly grazing beeves for the past ten or twelve miles.

The town itself was as full of trailhands as the countryside around it was full of beeves. Front Street between the saloons and the rails was a mass of horseflesh and humanity, the horses mostly standing more or less still and the humans mostly staggering from one beer parlor to the next.

The smells and the sounds coming out of the saloons were inviting after the dry ride down from Larned. But Front Street was entirely too full of people who might remember a man called Longarm. He wanted no one to question—not *too* closely, anyway—the past of a man who called himself Long Tom Custis.

So Longarm hurried past the busy, noisy, raucous attractions of Front Street and crossed to the other side of the tracks.

The stock pens, acre upon acre of them, some so new they had not yet had time for their timber to weather, stretched along the south side of the tracks. Uninhibited Front Street lay on the north side facing the rails. Respectable townspeople had their homes and even a few businesses to the north of Front, with most of the business district lying just east of the infamous saloons and honkytonks where the cash proceeds of a trail drive were so often left on "deposit." It was past all of these that Longarm rode, down beyond the bawling cattle in the loading pens to a shantytown strung out along the banks of the Arkansas

River. It was an area where people tended to sleep through the daylight hours and where questions were not welcome.

No one had ever bothered to lay out streets in the shantytown. Common usage had worn paths here and there among the shacks. Judging from the smell, no one bothered much with concerns about sanitation here either. The shacks themselves were flimsy affairs that would be no great loss whenever the slow-moving Arkansas got its dander up and came roaring up over its banks.

There were no stores, hotels, restaurants, or even proper saloons down here. Longarm was not even sure the area was considered to be a part of Dodge, whose leading citizens were lately beginning to make noises about respectability and decorum.

Longarm chose a shack that seemed to be a bit more stoutly built than its neighbors. It at least had some oiled paper tacked over the window openings. He pulled to a halt in front of it.

"Get the fuck out o' here," a voice rasped from inside the place.

Friendly crowd, Longarm thought. He dismounted and stood patiently with the reins trailing from his hand.

"Get out, I tol' you. We don't do no business this time o' day. A girl's got to sleep, y'know."

Longarm was interested to discover that a woman was doing the talking. He hadn't been able to tell from the whiskeyed voice.

"I'm not looking to do any business," Longarm said, and continued to wait.

A moment later the woman showed herself at the doorway. She had a pale complexion and bad teeth and held a pink wrapper clutched shut under her throat. His biggest impression was of the mass of tangled, brightly artificial red hair that frowsed like a thundercloud around her head. A man would have to be awfully drunk *and* the light awfully dim to want to pay for that one's services, Longarm thought uncharitably.

"Get out o' here, I tol' you. You wanta get laid, mister, you wait till a decent hour."

Longarm hadn't known there were decent hours, or indecent ones for that matter, for that particular activity. He supposed he should be grateful for the knowledge, but he was not.

"I didn't come here for that, and I'm sorry I disturbed you. I'm looking for a place to stay."

"Not here, you won't. Now get your ass gone before I call the police on you," the off-duty whore threatened.

Longarm laughed. It probably was not very polite of him, but he couldn't help it. The idea of the bawd calling a policeman, and to come down here at that, was too ludicrous to ignore.

The red-haired whore left the doorway in a huff, but her place was taken a moment later by a blinking, bleary-eyed, much smaller girl who might have been quite pretty if she had been decently dressed and seen in other circumstances. She gave Longarm a slow, uncertain look, then shrugged before she spoke. "You got any money, mister?"

"I already told your friend that I'm not looking for—"

"That isn't what I meant," she interrupted. "I mean, can you pay cash money for a place to stay?"

Longarm nodded.

The girl hesitated for only a moment, then said, "There's a lady—not one of us, mind—but there's a lady lives near here. Her man took off an' left her, an' I happen to know she don't want to turn out like me an' my friends here. I was thinking . . ."

"I could pay," Longarm said quickly. "Cash."

"I can't make you any promises, mind. But it might be a help to her."

Longarm nodded again.

The girl hesitated a moment longer, then stepped out into the sunlight, her wrapper pulled modestly close about her. "All right. I'll show you. But you got to promise to leave her be if she says no. Okay?"

"Okay," Longarm assured her.

The girl was thin and did not look healthy in the strong light of day, although he could still see a certain appeal that she must once have had, almost an innocence. He doubted that she was yet eighteen years old, but already she looked used-up and worn. She was young enough perhaps to have regrets, to still want to help some other woman avoid her own fate, but too long in the business to have any hope for herself. Longarm followed silently while she led the way upstream along a faint path to another miserable shack along the riverbank and rapped loudly on the doorjamb because there was no door there for her to knock on.

Chapter 3

A piece of old canvas was hung where the door should have been. The heavy cloth was pulled aside, and a young woman stepped outside.

She was pretty enough, or should have been. She really would have been quite attractive except for being so painfully thin and the fact that she had the unhealthy pallor of near starvation. Her hair, a light, almost blonde brown, was pinned neatly enough, but the front of her dress was unbuttoned and loose. She pulled it quickly closed when she saw Longarm, but even so its looseness gave Longarm the impression that this young woman—he guessed her to be in her very early twenties—might not be so far from the other women's occupation as his guide seemed to think. The dress she was wearing was a once-bright calico that had faded to a pale, dingy near-gray. Longarm let the young whore explain the reason for the visit.

"Oh, Lordy, yes," the woman whispered without hesitation. She did not even take the time to look Longarm over. "If you could pay me something...?"

"I could do that." He thought she was going to cry. For sure there was moisture making her eyes—very large, he noticed now, and a soft hazel in color—seem bright.

"How much?"

Longarm smiled at her. "Actually, ma'am, I kinda thought it was up to you to set the price you figure to charge."

"Oh. I suppose it is." She seemed flustered. She swiped quickly at her eyes with the back of her wrist. She hesitated. "I think... would two dollars..." She licked at her lips nervously. "Would that be too much?"

Longarm was torn. He was here trying to be a hard son of a bitch, on display for folks to notice and wonder about. So he couldn't come across as some kind of old-time knight on a white charger. But there was something about this young woman...

"Two dollars would be all right," he said, "and I supply whatever food I eat. Another two dollars a week if I can keep my horse in your shed over there." He carefully refrained from paying close attention to the pile of junk that was passing as a shed. It would take some fixing up before he would trust putting Tom Bradley's fine horse under that rickety roof.

The woman bobbed her head quickly. He suspected she did not trust herself to speak. Those few dollars apparently meant an awful lot to her. He was already thinking it was a shame that he did not expect to be here for long.

"Yes. Yes. Thank you. I... would you excuse me, sir? I have to finish feeding my baby." Her fingers fluttered nervously at the closed but still unbuttoned front of her dress. So she was nursing a little one. That explained the dishevelment.

"I'll tend to the horse while you do that."

"Yes, I..." she blushed inexplicably. "I am Anne

Crane. *Miss* Crane if you prefer." Her expression firmed and she raised her chin in proud defiance.

The young whore who had brought Longarm here looked surprised. Anne Crane told her, "He was never much of a man. All talk and flattery but no substance. I'll not have a child of mine bearing a false name, in particular that one." Her voice faltered for just a moment. "It isn't like we ever stood before a preacher, Katie. That was all just promises too."

Longarm felt embarrassed for her, although he had to admire her pluck. He turned away and led the horse toward the so-called shed without comment. There would be time enough later to tell her the lie about who he was.

And there sure would be more than enough time for her to nurse half a dozen infants before he would have that shed propped into some kind of usefulness for the animal.

"Mr. Custis."

"Yes, Miss Crane?"

"Be careful this evening."

"Why . . . yes. Uh, thank you."

That was certainly unexpected. She had hardly spoken to him while he was inside the shack arranging his things in the blanket-curtained cubicle she had set apart for him. Mostly she had spent her time in a corner fussing with a chubby, cooing, toothless little boy. The kid was a cute little bugger, Longarm had to admit.

When she had nursed the infant again—its name was James, for some reason known as Pippin—she had turned to face the corner and covered herself and the little boy with a clean diaper.

Longarm had not brought any food into the house as yet, so he would not have felt comfortable eating with Miss Crane and the kid, even if something had been offered. He suspected, but had not wanted to prowl in her things to find out for sure, that she had no food in the shack to offer. He would have to remember to do something about that while he was in town. And by now, coming evening, he was damned well hungry himself. He had not eaten since breakfast.

He pushed through the rough canvas door and found the path that led up to the activities of Dodge. Ahead of him he could see several small groups of gaudily-dressed whores also making the short hike up to their places of employment. He could have saddled Bradley's horse and ridden up, of course, but the distance was not far and Longarm frankly enjoyed the twilight walk with the heat of the day subsiding and a cool, fresh scent in the air. Then a puff of breeze came up, traveling first across the stock pens, and Longarm wondered if he shouldn't have brought the horse after all, to make the trip a quicker one.

He walked around the west end of the pens while the bawds took the shorter route past the depot on their way to Front Street. Longarm wanted to do some mingling, but noplace where he might be recognized, so he would have to avoid the usual watering holes.

Cowponies and rattling wagons flowed back and forth in the broad area between Front and the railroad. Someone down the street let out a holler that was about halfway between a Rebel yell and a Comanche war whoop, and that person or some other fired a revolver into the air. No one seemed to pay particular attention to either form of merry-making. It was coming night and Dodge City was having fun.

Longarm found a small, dimly lighted saloon on the fringes of the activity and went inside.

The place was tiny, primarily a plank bar stretched across the back wall with shelving and bottles and small kegs behind it. There were no tables to sit at and only a handful of customers. The place was relatively quiet. If it had a name it was not displayed anywhere that Longarm could see. The men who came here seemed to be interested in serious drinking instead of louder forms of hell-raising.

"I'll have a beer," Longarm told the barman. "And where's your free lunch?"

"You want a drink, put your money down. You want a meal, go somewheres else."

Longarm fixed the man with a stare, but the barkeep didn't blink. Nice fellow, Longarm thought. He turned and left the place. He could feel the hunger gnawing at his belly now. Thoughts of the free lunch spreads over on Front made his mouth water, but not so badly that he was willing to risk the job over them. He went to walking again, up the hill and around behind the familiar haunts like the Longbranch, beyond the back alleys, and down again to the business district of the town. That should be safe enough, he decided. At this time of evening the local peace officers who might remember him should be in busier neighborhoods than this.

He found a barbershop that had a line of drovers outside it waiting for their turn at the bath water. Beside the barbershop was a cafe that seemed to cater to cowhands. The steaks there were quick, cheap, and welcome. Longarm put himself around two of them before he hollered quit.

The other diners in the place were all men, all dressed in their wrinkled best, and all with slicked-down hair that smelled of bay rum. Obviously they were trailhands who had already had their turn at the bathtubs next door.

"Lose any on the way up?" Longarm asked the man sitting next to him.

"Not so many," the cowboy said around a mouthful of beef. "Gave away more'n we lost. The water an' the grass was mostly good the whole way. Good year for it, they say." He frowned. "Prob'ly why the market's off now. Too damn many cattle making it up the trail this year. Prices goin' down again, the way I hear it."

"Really?"

"Ayup. Or so they say. Pisses the boss off, but me, I don' care. I get paid the same regardless."

"There is that."

"Uh-huh." The man used his pocketknife to slice off another huge chunk of steak and crammed it into his mouth.

"Do they say when they expect the prices to go up again?"

The cowhand grunted and swallowed with a loud gulp. It was a wonder he did not choke himself on the thick wad of half-chewed meat. "Even I c'n figure that out." He grinned. "First herds next spring. Be good prices again then. Not likely until."

That was logical enough, although in truth the price of beef on the hoof still was quite good, just not as high as it had been a few months earlier. Longarm wondered if that basic fact of the cow business had anything to do with the reason he was here.

"Like you say," Longarm mused, "the working stiff gets his few pennies whether the price is good or not."

"Yeah." The man dug at his steak with the knife again. Judging from the crust clinging to the back of the blade, he used the same implement to clean his horses' hooves. "But I can't complain. I ride for Tull an' Johnston from down east of Beeville. They're on the square, the both of them. If you know what I mean."

Longarm knew, but was not a participant. Besides, a man like Long Tom Custis would not be expected to know. So he let it slide, and the talkative cowhand moved past the remark as if it had been of no importance.

"Anyways, they promised a bonus if we didn't lose but so many head. So we'll collect on that sure. Good men. If they say it, it's so."

"Good to ride for an outfit like that," Longarm agreed.

"Who you with?" The man carefully trimmed some fat off the edge of his steak and crammed that under his moustache with a sigh of pleasure.

"I'm loose right now. Paid off after the herd got here."

"Tull an' Johnston, they're awful good. Keep you right on for the down ride if you want to stick with the outfit. Course, you can pay off here if you want. Me, I'm stickin'."

"I don't blame you." Longarm fingered his chin for a

moment, then said, "Say, I got an old pard that rides for an outfit down close to your home country. At least I think it's close. Place name of Tilden."

The drover nodded. "That's over in McMullen County. I know of it."

"You wouldn't happen to know if the Holcroft outfit's in town, would you?"

It was the drover's turn to stroke his chin. "Holcroft? Holcroft. No. That don't ring no bells. Don't think I've ever heard of them. Course, I'm not all that familiar with that part o' the country. It ain't all that far, but it's the wrong direction for us to go chasin' come the winter drift. We mostly run our hunts down toward the coast. What brand, though? I'd more likely know the brand than the man anyhow."

Longarm shook his head. "Don't know. Hell, I could even be wrong about the name. It's just a hear-tell. Haven't seen my friend since we worked the Jinglebob together. But that was a while back."

"The Jinglebob? Hell, I know a fella worked there for a spell. Name of Hank Dortneuf. You know him?"

Longarm frowned in thought. "I recall a fella named Hank, but I disremember his last name. Just a kid, built about as big around as the wiping stick out of a squirrel rifle." Longarm smiled as the old memories came back. "I don't remember much about him, but that kid could throw a *pial* prettier'n anybody I ever saw, before or since."

The drover laughed and slapped his leg. "Shit, that's ol' Hank all right. But I reckon it has been a while back. Hank's got him a belly that likes to hide his damn saddle-horn now. If the man didn't rope tie-fast he couldn't make no living these days. But he c'n still make a rope stand up an' do tricks when he lets a loop roll. How's about that."

"Is Hank with Tull and Johnston too?" Longarm was damn sure hoping that he was not. If there was anything he did not need right now, it was old acquaintances.

"Sure as shit is," the drover said happily.

Longarm felt his gut tighten.

"Wisht you and him could get together again. But Hank let a damned Palouse horse carry him over a cutbank just before we left. I told him he shouldn't trust one of them sons o' bitches. Toughest fuckers I ever seen, but the dumbest too. And you know old Hank. Once he gets his mind set on something, he don't know enough to quit." The drover cackled. "Kinda like me, come to think of it, except even I know enough not to trust one o' them bastards. Anyways, ol' Hank is laid up back to Beeville, so you'll miss seein' him again."

"I'm sorry to hear that," Longarm lied. He shoved his empty plate away and stood. "Next year," he said. "Tell Hank I was asking after him."

"I'll do that," the drover mumbled around a mouthful of beef.

Longarm turned and got the hell out of there quick, before the drover remembered that he did not know Longarm's name. Tom Custis would have meant nothing to Hank Dortneuf, and Longarm sure did not want to start spreading the name of Custis Long around Dodge City.

The drover sputtered some sounds behind Longarm's quickly retreating back, his efforts hampered by the load of steak in his jaws, but Longarm pretended he did not hear and made it safely out into the street.

Chapter 4

"Holcroft? Sure, I know him." The man's voice was carefully neutral, perhaps a little guarded, Longarm thought, as if he held an opinion but wanted to shield it, whatever it might be.

They were standing between the railroad tracks and the loading chutes while a shipment of longhorns was being loaded onto cars for transport back to the packing houses of Kansas City. It was dark enough, except for the light of a few men with bullseye lanterns, that Longarm did not likely have to be worried about being recognized. The man he was talking with had been pointed out to him as a cattle buyer, presumably here to supervise the shipment of beeves he had purchased on someone's behalf, or maybe even his own.

The buyer, who said his name was Murphy, turned his head and gave Longarm another look. He did not, however, seem to find anything discomforting about Longarm's rough clothing.

That was one nice thing about dealing with cattlemen and cattle brokers. They tended to make no assumptions about a man simply because of the way he chose to dress, particularly at the end of a long and difficult trail. The roughest-looking, foulest-talking, most gun-laden ranny might turn out to be the biggest he-coon in whatever neck of the woods he ventured out of. They said that old Shanghai Pierce was often mistaken, particularly when he neglected to put his teeth in, for a mush-mouthed old saloon swamper. But they also said that old Mr. Pierce owned half the beeves in south Texas. And those he didn't already own he was about to.

Since Murphy had not volunteered any information about Holcroft, Longarm put another question to him. "Is the man in town now?"

Murphy shook his head, paying more attention to the loading process than to the tall man who stood beside him. "Just a second," Murphy said. He shouted to get the attention of the loading crew foreman, who was having some difficulty convincing the next pen of cattle that they should leave that confinement and exchange it for the uncertainties of a closed boxcar. "Quit trying to prod them out like that, Frank. You're just making them nervous. Fetch that Judas steer and use him."

The foreman waved and turned to pass the word to his handlers. The men left the gate open to the loading chute but quit trying to force the beeves into it. The foreman led a docile steer out of a nearby pen, brought it to the open gate where the still nervous longhorns were balking, and let them see and smell the newcomer. Then he led the tame steer quickly up into the waiting cattle car.

The half-wild longhorns, calmed by seeing another bovine creature so willing to enter the car, followed behind the Judas and were soon loaded. Then the foreman came back down the ramp, still leading the Judas.

"Okay, boss," the foreman called. Already his handlers had opened the connecting gates between the maze of pens, and a new load of cattle was being herded into the last pen before the loading chute. A trainman waved a lantern, and up forward the engineer began to drag the next empty cattle car into position at the chute ramp. It was a smooth and efficient process, repeated day and night during the shipping season here.

"That's better," Murphy rumbled to himself. "Keep up that horseshit and they'll sweat off ten pound of tallow from every head they load."

"Uh-huh," Longarm agreed.

"Oh. Yeah. You were asking me something."

"Holcroft," Longarm repeated. "Is he in town?"

"No, but he will be soon. His wife's already here. That means he won't be far behind. He never leaves her be for very long."

"Really?"

Murphy nodded. "Can't say as I blame him. Used to be some looker, that one. Still is, for that matter." The buyer smiled. "If I was just a few years older I think I'd try and take her away from Joe my own self."

"Holcroft will be bringing a herd in soon, then?" Longarm asked, deliberately giving an impression of ignorance.

Murphy snorted. "Huh. I only wish he was. He used to do that, mind. But that was when he was in the business of raising them himself. Went belly up in the business, though they say that's hard to do in south Texas. No, Mr. Custis—"

"Call me Tom," Longarm interrupted.

"All right, Tom. But no, what Joe is doing nowadays is taking cattle *away* from Dodge, not bringing them to it."

"He's brokering?" Longarm asked, again pretending to misunderstand.

Murphy snorted again and this time shook his head as well. "Tom, I really can't figure *what* Joe is up to. What he's doing is plain old droving."

"Away from Dodge?"

"That's right. Away from Dodge and away from the railroad too. Taking herds on consignment here and driving them west, then up that new public road to Ogallala, up in Nebraska. That's on the Union Pacific tracks, of course, so from there he can sell them and ship them across to the Chicago packers."

"That makes sense enough," Longarm said, "if the Chicago plants are paying better than the KC packers."

Murphy snorted so hard he had to wipe his nose afterward. "That's what makes no sense, Tom," the man said. "They aren't."

"Really?"

"Oh, I don't say the price isn't better. But the difference is usually fifty to seventy-five cents. I don't think I've ever seen it more than a dollar different. And that's per head, now, not per hundredweight. At the best, maybe a dollar better than the Kansas City price. Mostly not even that."

"Yeah, but if you figure a dollar a head better price, and herds of—what?—three thousand head?—then he has to be making a profit on the deal."

Murphy muttered something that Longarm could not hear. He probably didn't want to anyway. "You still don't understand, Tom. Let me explain it." That was exactly what Longarm was wanting him to do. He had already gotten one viewpoint on the deal from Billy Vail. He wanted a Dodge City cattle broker's opinion too.

"You got to remember, Tom, that no cowman is going to just up and turn his beeves over to Joe Holcroft or anyone else in exchange for the same money he could get from selling his cattle himself, right here, to me or one of the other buyers in town. You got that?"

Longarm nodded dutifully.

"Joe—and, mind you, I've done business with Joe in the past, used to consider him a friend, even—Joe guarantees the owners a profit increase of at least fifty cents a head. And like you already obviously know, the best size

32

herd to drive and manage is three thousand head. That means an increased profit of fifteen hundred dollars on the average herd. And I don't know of too many men who will pass up an extra fifteen hundred that they don't even have to work for. It's like he's promising them free money."

"It sure sounds good," Longarm agreed.

"But there's things about it that I for *sure* can't understand myself, Tom, and believe me I've given it some thought."

"Such as?"

"The first and the biggest thing is that Holcroft makes that promise, and he does it in writing, based on the herd count *leaving* Dodge City. Never mind the count when they get to Ogallala. Holcroft is gambling that him and his men can get every head of every herd all the way up to the UP tracks and sell them there at a profit. Now, personally, I've never known any bunch of drovers so good that they can guarantee against prairie-dog holes and quicksand, but that's just about what Holcroft is doing. Him and his men. Which is another thing. He has to be paying that trail crew of his. So their wages have to come out of his profits. If any. And, like I said, there are times when the Chicago price of beef won't be but fifty cents higher than the Kansas City price. And of course he's already pledged that amount to the owners of the cattle. So on a drive like that, he has to pay his wages and supplies and any losses right out of pocket. Even when the price is a full dollar higher in Chicago, he wouldn't make but a few cents for his time and trouble. But he does it. Been doing it time after time and herd after herd, this whole shipping season."

"But he does pay off the increased profit?"

Murphy nodded. "Herd after herd, the whole summer long. Each and every time. Some of the owners have waited here for their checks. I've talked to them while they were waiting, and I've talked to them after they got their money. No one has ever yet lost a cent by letting Joe Holcroft take his cattle on to Ogallala."

"It sounds like a good deal for them," Longarm said.

"Sure. But a dumb one for Joe Holcroft. And Joe never struck me as being foolish. Sure, he went broke down in Texas. Lost everything he had down there, one way or another. I never heard the details and don't need to. The fact is, I've done business with Holcroft. He never struck me as stupid. So there is damn sure *something* about this Ogallala deal that I'm not seeing. And I have to tell you, Tom, it damn near drives me nuts trying to figure out what. If anybody ever does figure it, I'd sure like to hear what it is, because it's making me think I don't understand the cow business near as well as I pretend to."

"I thank you for the information, Mr. Murphy."

"Surely."

"You said Mrs. Holcroft is in town and that should mean that Joe will be back soon?"

"That's right. She doesn't like to go with the herd on the drives, so she takes the rails and a stage connection up to Ogallala when they leave here and is there waiting for the herds to arrive. Then when they head back this way with the wagon and remuda to pick up another herd, she comes down ahead of them again. I saw her in the lobby of the Grand this afternoon, so I know Joe and his crew won't be far behind. It doesn't take them but a day or three longer when they don't have to push cattle, maybe three weeks for the trip going up to Nebraska. They ought to be here in three more days at the longest."

"I do thank you, Mr. Murphy."

"That's all ri—" Murphy broke off in the middle of the word and leaned forward to shout at his foreman again. "Damn it, Frank, quit fretting the tallow off those critters. Bring the Judas steer around again, will you?"

Longarm reached into his pocket for a cheroot and bit the tip off it, thinking as he walked. Everything Murphy had told him checked precisely with what Billy Vail had said back in Denver.

The point was, though, that it was not the government's

responsibility to keep a man from being a damn fool. If Joe Holcroft wanted to lose money in the droving business, the man was entitled to do so.

Billy had said himself that no one had ever lost money on the deal except maybe Holcroft. And there was nothing illegal about that.

If Longarm hadn't had that softly whispered conversation with Henry before he left the office, he might well think that Billy was losing more out of his head than just his hair.

As it was, well, even Longarm might not be able to object if or when the U. S. Attorney decided it was time they had some new faces in the federal marshal's office. Down to and including certain deputies whom Deputy Marshal Custis Long did not care to name.

The saloon was a little busier than it had been before dinner. It had not improved any while he was away, though. The best thing that could be said about it was that the lighting was dim. Probably the owner of the place was too tight-fisted to spend any more than he absolutely had to on lamp oil. So there was less danger of recognition here for Longarm than there would have been in any of the better places. Longarm found an open space at the plank bar and moved into it. The bartender gave no indication that he had ever laid eyes on Longarm before.

"Maryland rye," Longarm ordered.

"I got rye. No idea where it come from."

"All right then, rye. Wherever it came from."

"Half a bit. In advance." The barman did not move toward his shelves until Longarm had laid a quarter on the bar.

"I'll take both halves now," Longarm said. Otherwise the skinflint bastard would give him twelve cents change for the half-bit drink and demand thirteen cents in payment when the refill was ordered.

Even then the bartender saved himself the price of a

speck of soap—assuming, which it might not be safe to do, that the man bothered to use any soap when he washed his glasses—by pouring both shots into one glass. The amazement there was that the fellow used glasses at all instead of the more durable tinware. He must have gotten a hell of a bargain on them, Longarm thought.

"Thanks," Longarm said sarcastically. The bartender ignored the tone, if he even noticed it.

Longarm tasted the rye. He raised an eyebrow and tasted it again. It was Maryland, by damn, and about as good as a man could hope to find. As mellow on his tongue as the smoke from a ten-cent cigar. He took another swallow and another and laid down a second quarter.

The only explanation, Longarm concluded, was that the barkeep was buying stolen merchandise on the double-cheap. There wasn't any other way a man like that could stock something so fine.

"Again?" the barman asked.

Longarm nodded.

Most of the other men in the place were putting their money down for beer or for the bar-run whiskey, which looked and smelled no better than Injun whiskey made from trade alcohol and tobacco plugs. Longarm felt like he'd uncovered a mother lode.

"You wouldn't have a bottle of that that a man could buy, would you?"

"Got a whole quarter-keg of the shit if you want to pay the price for it."

"A bottle will do me."

The barman grunted and pulled an emptied bottle out of the trash barrel behind the bar.

"Rinse it out first, will you?"

The bartender scowled but did as the customer asked. "Two dollars," he said, as cheerful and friendly as ever. Longarm laid a pair of cartwheels on the bar, and the barkeep shuffled them into a pocket of his apron before he set the bottle down.

"Thanks." Longarm picked up the corked jug and turned to leave. It was time he headed back for the shanty. Holcroft was not in town, and Longarm still had some shopping to do before he took the path back to his rented quarters.

A man just entering the place looked Longarm full in the face and then barged straight ahead into him, knocking the bottle of rye from his hand and sending it crashing to the floor in an explosion of broken glass and good-smelling rye whiskey.

"Watch where you're going, asshole," the newcomer snarled.

Longarm looked from the broken bottle of rye to the rude bastard's face and back again. The man was big and bearded and rather obviously in a foul humor. He was just as obviously drunk.

Under other circumstances, Longarm might have made some allowances for the influence of already consumed liquor. But, after all, Long Tom Custis needed to establish something of a reputation here.

"Asshole?" Longarm asked mildly. "Mighty clever of you, mister, the way you can form words when you fart."

The big man's face flushed with trigger-quick anger. Men on either side of the two must have heard the exchange, because there was a sudden interest in the extreme ends of the bar, with men from the middle section hurrying to crowd over to the sides.

"Fight!" someone yelped, and more men who had been outside began trying to crowd through the door so they could watch.

"Fight?" the big man growled. "I'm not gonna fight ol' limberdick here. I'm gonna blow his fucking head off." He reached drunkenly for the butt of his revolver.

There was an easy response Longarm could take to that, of course, and no one would have faulted him for it. The big drunk was hard on the prod and asking for it.

On the other hand, while there were a good many things

an undercover peace officer could reasonably do to help him establish a cover story, killing local drunks would be considered an extreme method.

Longarm took a step forward and snatched the revolver —a nearly useless and not even cartridge-converted old LeMat—out of the drunk's hand. He looked at the relic, shook his head, and tossed the thing aside. Someone in the crowd sniggered.

It took a moment for the drunk to realize that he had been disarmed. Awareness and fury spread over his broad face in a slow flood of expression.

"Damn you . . ."

Longarm hit him.

The drunk staggered backward several paces and blinked. Blood was beginning to flow from his nose and spread down into his beard. He blinked a few times more and charged forward.

A wild overhand right battered Longarm's guard aside and landed with a ringing thump over Longarm's left ear.

Longarm stepped inside the drunk's flailing arms and pounded a sharp tattoo on the big man's belly.

That should have ended it. Generally speaking, a drunk receiving that kind of massage would become more interested in puking than in fighting. Longarm knew that. Apparently the big man didn't.

The man wasn't just drunk. He was also about as tough as chrome-tanned latigo. He ignored the beating Longarm thought he was delivering and wrapped his arms in a bearhug around his slimmer opponent, locking his wrists behind Longarm's back and applying an unexpected, rib-threatening pressure.

"Oh, shit," Longarm mumbled.

If anyone heard, they ignored him. More men had crowded into the place to watch the show. They were shouting encouragement indiscriminately to both parties, and someone with a loud voice seemed to be taking bets.

The shouted odds seemed to be very much in the drunk's favor.

Longarm raised a knee out to the side and stomped down with his boot heel, trying to rake the big son of a bitch's shin and make him break the hold. The only problems with that were that the drunk moved his leg out of the way, and Longarm, forgetting the unaccustomed length of those damned Mexican spurs, managed to rake his own left calf instead with the rowels of the spurs.

"Aw, shit," Longarm repeated, louder this time and with more feeling.

That feeling of disgust—and of a certain amount of pain in his leg—was close to being all the feeling Longarm had left.

The big bastard was powerful. What little Longarm could make out in front of his eyes was beginning to sway and waver, and there seemed to be a misty red fog covering everything in the room.

He tried a knee again, this time aiming for the drunk's crotch, but the big man actually laughed as he easily turned it with his thigh. He chuckled and snorted and bore down harder with that bone-crunching grip.

"He's got 'im!" someone shouted. "Dave's got 'im now." No one seemed to be cheering for the stranger any longer.

Longarm tried to grab hold of Dave's cods, but he could not reach that far south. He could not reach hardly anything, in fact, with both arms pinned tight to his sides inside the iron-like circle of Dave's arms.

Do with what you've got, Longarm told himself.

He turned his palms outward and grabbed hold of whatever cloth and flesh he could find, and pinched. Hard. Squeezed for all he was worth.

"Sumbitch!" Dave hollered.

"Yeah," Longarm said. He immediately regretted the loss of breath, but it was too late to recall.

"Quit that." Dave tried to wriggle away from the insistent pinching of his belly.

A tiny gap opened between the two bodies. It wasn't much, but it let Longarm gulp in some fresh air.

Dave jerked Longarm back and forth, shaking him like a terrier with a rat. Longarm lost his grip on Dave's belly, but got another deep breath of fresh air in exchange. It seemed a fair enough swap at the time.

Dave grabbed at him again, trying to tighten the hold for the kill, but Longarm was able to drop a few inches toward the floor before Dave's arms closed.

Longarm found himself with Dave's bearhug around his shoulders—*much* better than around his ribs—and with his nose pressed flat against Dave's chest. It would have been nice if Dave had stopped in at that barbershop for a bath on his way here.

The contact did not last long. Longarm's hands hung lower now. And he was no longer having trouble with his breathing.

Grinning into the grimy front of Dave's shirt, Longarm shoved his hand forward into the crotch of Dave's jeans and took another firm hold.

He clamped down as hard as he was able and drove up hard and fast onto his toes.

Dave screamed and pitched backward, losing his hold on Longarm.

"That's better," Longarm muttered. He stood waiting while Dave climbed woozily back onto his feet.

This time Longarm knew better than to let the burly drunk close on him. When Dave came forward, Longarm extended his fist with the knuckles forward and slugged the drunk in the throat.

This time Dave did what he should have done a while ago when Longarm was pounding on his belly. He went chalk-white in the face, pitched down onto his knees, and began to spew up everything he had had to eat and drink lately.

Longarm stepped aside and turned back to the bar. "I'll need another bottle of that rye," he said. He tried to say it calmly, but he suspected there was some gasping and panting heard that would interfere with the effect he wanted.

The bartender fetched another empty bottle out of the barrel, and this time he rinsed it without being asked. He shook his head. "First time I ever seen that," he said. "First time I know of Dave being whipped."

"He was drunk," Longarm said.

"Shit, man, that's the onliest time he fights is when he's drunk."

"Gentle fella when he's sober, is he?"

"Shit, no. Meanest son of a bitch you ever seen when he's sober. Drunk is when he's feeling playful enough to fight a man fair. But I ain't never seen nor heard of him being whipped, whether drunk or sober."

Longarm paid a second time for his bottle of rye whiskey and got the hell out of there.

Chapter 5

"I hope you don't mind, ma'am—I mean, miss—but I brought a bottle of liquor with me. I can take it out to the shed if that bothers you." That was not the sort of thing Long Tom Custis should have said, but Longarm did not think of that until it was too late. Besides, he honestly did not want to offend the young woman.

"I don't mind, Mr. Custis."

"Good." He set the small crate down on her table, plucked his bottle of Maryland rye out of it, and took that into the blanket-curtained area that had been set aside as his bedroom. He went back into the main part of the one-room shanty.

Miss Crane had already prepared herself for bed while he was away, likely grateful for the privacy his absence afforded her. She had her hair down and loose and was wearing a thin wrapper. The baby was asleep on a pallet that she likely would share later.

"I brought some food, ma'am . . . miss." With the infant sleeping in the corner over there, Longarm was having a bit of trouble remembering that distinction. "I said I'd provide food for the household, so you should make yourself free with it."

She swallowed hard when she looked at the box of things he had brought. He suspected that she was salivating with hunger. Probably she had been slighting her own needs of late, although she continued to provide milk for the babe. A thing like that was hard on a woman, Longarm knew. It was no wonder she was so scrawny.

"Would you . . . would you like me to fix something for you now, Mr. Custis?"

Longarm's first thought was of refusal. He was not hungry, having eaten his fill and then some at the restaurant in town. But he looked at her again and saw the way she kept looking at the box. There was a slab of bacon poking up along one side and a sack of cornmeal and some cans of things he had found at the store. Proud as this Anne Crane seemed to be, he suspected she might refuse to cook anything for herself if he went on to bed.

"That would be nice, ma'am."

"All right." She bent to check on the infant, then took some dry slats of scantling from a woodbox beside the stove and tried to light a fire using flint and tinder.

"Let me do that, ma'am." Longarm held a splinter in the meager flame of a grease lamp that provided the only light in the place and used it to start the stove. Anne Crane was more stubborn than clear-thinking at this point, he thought.

"D'you have a woodpile, ma'am, so I could bring in more wood for that box?"

She shook her head. "I gather . . . whatever I can. Whatever I can find."

Longarm made a mental note to see what he could scrounge for fuel come daylight. He also reminded himself to bring some coal oil for light. There was a lamp hanging on the wall, but either it was empty or she had too little oil to waste. The grease lamp she was using was only a dish of rancid tallow with a twist of cotton scrap in it for a wick.

"What would you like for your supper, Mr. Custis?"

"Nothing fancy," he said. "Whatever you care to fix."

"I haven't any lard, but I could fry some bacon and use the drippings to make some cornbread. Would that be all right?"

"Yes, ma'am." He gave up trying to correct himself to the proper form of address.

"It won't be very long."

Longarm went behind his blanket and helped himself to a pull on the rye jug, then went out to check on Tom Bradley's horse. The neighborhood was not one to inspire trust, but nothing in the shed seemed to have been disturbed. But then, he had carried his saddle and gear inside the shack earlier and left only the horse and smelly saddle blanket out where they would be vulnerable to prowlers.

When Longarm went back inside the bacon, a single helping of it, was cooling on a plate, and Miss Crane had cornbread baking in a Dutch oven on top of the stove. The stove was too cheap a model to have a proper oven built into it.

"It shan't be long now, Mr. Custis. I put coffee on too. Is that all right?"

"Just fine, ma'am." She had put out only a single cup on the table, so he fetched another from a shelf over the stove and set it down too, then put beside the cups a can of condensed milk and a sack of sugar to lace the brew with. The sugar and milk would be good energy for her, and he could stand taking his that way this one time too so as to make her feel better about using the supplies he had really brought just for her.

"You'll join me, of course," he said when she put the meal in front of him.

"Oh, but I . . ."

"I'm really not very hungry. Had a bite in town a while

ago and now I'm not nearly as hungry as I'd thought."

"If you . . ."

"I do."

Once she sat down to the food she tucked into it in a hurry. Longarm had a single strip of bacon and one small piece of the cornbread for the sake of appearance and let her finish the rest.

He was amazed that she could get around so much so fast. But not at all surprised when a minute or so after she got red in the face and embarrassed-looking. Without a word she rushed outside. He could hear her running around toward the back of the shanty.

That told him where the outhouse was, anyway. That was another sure sign that she had been long empty. A person who hasn't had food for a while, not near to the point of starvation but longer than is normal, can still eat a fair amount, but the stuff tends to run right through when they do eat again.

That wasn't the sort of thing he could discuss with a woman he barely knew, though, and neither of them commented when she returned.

She did look a little hangdog, though, he thought. And she seemed more than a mite nervous. She was sighing a lot and seemed disinclined toward small talk.

"Is there something wrong, ma'am?"

She shook her head much too quickly and much too severely for him to believe the denial.

Longarm yawned and stretched. "It's been a long day, ma'am. I'll turn in now. Thank you for the supper." He stood. "Uh, you won't mind if I have a smoke before I got to sleep, will you?"

"What?" She looked surprised, and still very nervous. "I mean . . . no. I wouldn't mind at all." Her eyes dropped away from his and she looked like she was going to cry. "You won't . . . I mean, during the night?" A tear-track slid down the hollow planes of her cheek and glistened in the low light. "I shouldn't want my baby to see . . . anything."

46

Longarm was confused for a moment. Then he realized what she was afraid of. She fully expected him to demand payment for those few scraps of food she had eaten. She actually expected him to come at her during the night.

"Miss Crane."

"Yes?" She still did not look at him.

"You've been in hard company of late, I'd guess. But there's all kinds of men inside, I mean in the ways they think and the ways they do, just like there's all kinds on the outside, short or tall or fair or hairy. All kinds. You should remember that."

"My . . . my father was a good man. In his way. But I ran off. An' now I've come to this."

"There's more men like your pa, Miss Crane, than there are like the one that left you here."

"Are you like my father, Mr. Custis?" She still did not look at him.

"No. Your pa is likely a better man than I am in the ways that truly count. But I try not to be any worse'n I am. Good night, Miss Crane."

"Good night, Mr. Custis."

He could hear her for quite a long time working slowly at the dishwashing and cleaning up, and it was some time after that before she finally blew out the flame from her grease lamp and joined the infant on the pallet.

Longarm made a slow and wary approach to the cafe. It was the poorest and greasiest one he could find, way to hell and gone off at the fringes of the business district, and a place where it was most unlikely he would see anyone he knew in Dodge. But now he not only had to worry about being spotted by old friends and casual acquaintances, he also wanted to avoid that Tull and Johnston drover who had been so talkative the night before. This business of having to sneak around the town and try to do a job without being seen and recognized was a pain. He hoped that buyer was right and the Holcroft crowd would not be long in arriving.

The cafe, poor as it looked, was nearly full at this time of morning. That was a good sign. Longarm was hungry enough to eat boiled rattlesnake buttons. He was always ready enough for a meal in the morning, and today it was worse because he'd had to pick and prowl around the edges of a perfectly good breakfast once already and then leave nearly all of it behind so Miss Crane would have plenty of leftovers to feed herself. What he'd eaten had only put a fine edge on his appetite, and now he was ready for a peck of anything that was hot and mostly edible.

"Twenty cents for the full meal," the waiter told him. "Ten for oatmeal an' coffee."

"I'll have the whole deal." Longarm selected a seat on a bench at the rearmost table where he could keep an eye on the door and the traffic beyond it. He thought about lighting a cheroot, but his breakfast was delivered before he could do so and he put his attention onto that instead.

Luke Short and a local deputy walked past on the sidewalk. Longarm had met the young deputy before but couldn't remember his name now; Masters or something like that. They had a big-nosed but otherwise not too unattractive woman between them and were paying attention to her, fortunately. Longarm ducked his head to avoid accidental eye contact with them, and they passed on without noticing him. He muttered a few curses under his breath.

"It's all right," somebody beside him whispered. "They're gone now."

"What?"

"The deppity. He's gone now. Didn't spot you."

"Thanks."

The man who had spoken to him was no one Longarm recalled seeing before. He didn't look like much. Just another hand with a saddle shine on the seat of his jeans and cowshit on his boots. But he was obviously more observant than he appeared. And there was no dust or oxidation showing on the dark steel of the revolver he wore on his belt. "Thanks," Longarm repeated.

The man grinned at him and nodded. "Goose Coe is what they call me."

"Goose?"

"Believe me, you don't wanta hear all that."

"All right. They call me Tom Custis. Long Tom if you'd rather."

"Good to meetcha, Tom."

"Likewise, Goose." Longarm noticed that the good Mr. Coe had used the convention of the time and said that Coe was what he was called. He hadn't made any claims to that being his name. The distinction was one that not every cowhand would appreciate.

They chatted idly while both men finished eating. Then Longarm offered to buy Coe a drink to cut the grease of the fried breakfast.

"I could stand that, Tom. Thankee." Coe grinned. "I know a hog ranch down the way where a man won't be bothered by unpleasant comp'ny." He cut his eyes toward the sidewalk where the deputy had passed.

"Mighty nice of you, Goose." Longarm paid for his meal and followed Coe outside.

The sun was fully up now and pouring its heat onto the dusty streets of Dodge. Down the way, Front Street was alive and roaring. Coe turned the other way, though, and led Longarm past a block of boarding houses and on to a district of shacks almost as rickety and run-down as those along the river.

There was little activity at this end of town. A mongrel bitch lay in the thin shade of a dust-covered lilac bush nursing a litter of pups. Up ahead there was the sound of an axe head thunking into wood chunks.

"I hope you don't mind walking," Coe apologized, "but my friends and me got in kinda late last night, and my horse is most used up."

"I don't mind," Longarm assured him.

They walked on to the very edge of the town and turned north onto a path. The saloon—Longarm was not sure it merited the dignity of being called a saloon, actually—looked like a two-bit whore's crib that had degenerated below even that purpose. There was no telling what kind of rotgut would be served in a place like that.

Longarm didn't find out, either.

From behind them there was the soft scrape of feet rushing through the fine dust of the path.

Longarm whirled, his Colt in his fist without conscious thought. Beside him Goose Coe was almost as quick. Both men crouched at the ready with revolvers in their hands.

It was that big son of a bitch from the night before. Dave, they had called him.

He had to be sober by now. The bartender had said he was mean when he was dry, and he was sure as hell coming on mean right now.

His face was flushed dark red with fury, and he was breathing heavily. There was an ugly look of grim determination on him, and he ran silently toward Longarm with a double-bitted axe upraised and ready to strike.

There was no question at all that he intended to use it. If Longarm and Coe had not heard him coming he could have—and Longarm genuinely believed would have—split Longarm's skull apart like a ripe apple under the filed blade of that gleaming axe head.

He was only a few paces distant and too intent on his charge to stop or even to slow when Longarm and Coe turned to face him.

Longarm fired.

The Colt bellowed and bucked in his hand, and a damp red spot appeared on Dave's chest. The big man stumbled but kept coming, and that axe was still poised to strike.

Longarm fired again, and two more wet patches dimpled the front of Dave's shirt. Longarm was vaguely aware of the smoke and flame of Coe's revolver beside him.

Dave's legs lost their drive. He pitched face forward onto the ground. He lost his grip on the axe handle as he fell, and the heavy tool whipped blade over handle through the air like an overgrown tomahawk.

Longarm ducked to the side. The hickory shaft of the axe handle caromed painfully off the point of his shoulder, deflected high into the air, and fell with a thud into the dirt. Longarm was not paying any attention to it, though. His concentration was on Dave's body. If the big bastard moved . . .

Goose Coe straightened from the crouch he was still in. He let out his breath in a slow whistle and jammed his revolver back into his holster.

"Yeah," Longarm agreed.

Off in the direction of downtown Longarm could hear the shrill tweet of a police whistle.

Here there was no one else in sight. Just the dead man and the two live ones standing over him. Anyone inside the saloon seemed inclined to stay where they were.

"If you don't mind, Goose, I'll buy you that drink some other time."

Coe grinned at him. "Good. I was beginning to think maybe I'd done something to that feller an' couldn't even remember it. Glad to know my memory ain't goin' *that* bad."

"I'll see you later, then, Goose. And thanks for the help."

"Any time, Tom." Coe did not seem at all disturbed by the interruption. He certainly did not appear to be distressed by the sight of the dead body.

Coe ambled on toward the saloon, and Longarm turned and loped away up the path. He found a narrow alley between two shacks and ducked into it, then made his way carefully for several blocks before he turned back toward the railroad.

By then the local law had already rumbled past, puffing on their whistles as they ran. Longarm had often wondered what the reasoning was with those damnfool whistles. The only thing they did was to warn criminals that the officers were approaching.

51

Maybe that was the idea after all—to make damn sure there was no one left around to take shots at the officers. Not efficient, maybe, but mighty safe.

Longarm made his way across the tracks and back toward the other end of town. To all outward appearances he was just another cowhand in Dodge.

He had just killed a citizen of the community, of course, and eventually he would have to clear that up. In the meantime Dave's death would just have to go on the books as another murder by person or persons unknown, because the alternative would have meant exposure as a federal officer. Longarm suspected that the deceased's character did not warrant a confession and inquest at the expense of this assignment.

And Longarm frankly doubted that Goose Coe or any of his friends back at that saloon were going to be doing much talking to the local deputies. That was the kind of neighborhood where no one ever saw or heard a thing he didn't have to.

Longarm made a mental note to make the appropriate explanations when he could, and went on his way.

Chapter 6

"Yeah, he got in sometime last night, but I haven't seen him yet this morning. That's his missus going into the dining room now. You could ask her." The desk clerk nodded in the direction of the double doors that separated the lobby of the hotel from the attached restaurant. On the other side of the lobby was a smoking room for gentlemen only, and behind that was a smaller area where drinks were served and cards and tables were available.

The woman the clerk pointed out was standing with her back to Longarm. He could not see her face but her posture and carriage spoke wordlessly of self-assurance and beauty and quite possibly of money as well.

Her gown and matching bonnet were dark blue velvet, obviously expensive, and the trim of the dress matched the parasol that she carried furled under her arm. Her hair was done up in a tidy roll, dark and lightly streaked with hints of silver. While Longarm watched, a waiter hurried to greet her, bowed low, and led her into the restaurant with a flourish that was positively obsequious.

Longarm removed his battered black Kossuth hat and went to the doorway. The same waiter who had been in such a hurry to welcome Kathleen Holcroft took his time about greeting Longarm.

"I need to have a word with the lady." Longarm looked past the waiter to where Mrs. Holcroft was seated with a silver pot and china cup at her elbow and a huge menu spread out on the table before her. Longarm did not have to specify which lady. At this hour it was late for breakfast and early for lunch. The dining room was empty except for Mrs. Holcroft.

The waiter gave Longarm a slow and thorough inspection before answering. The man's attitude was just short of insulting. Distaste for seedy, sweat-smelling cowhands tugged the corners of his lips thin.

"Let me put it this way, sonny," Longarm said, although the waiter was probably half a dozen years older than Longarm. "You take me over there just like you ought, or I'll pick you up an' stuff you upside-down into that big ol' fern pot in the corner. An' then I'll go over an' talk to the lady anyhow."

The waiter gulped rather loudly and motioned for the guest to follow. Longarm thought the fellow had begun to sweat a bit before they reached the table where Mrs. Holcroft was still examining her menu.

"My apologies, madam," the waiter said with another low bow. "A . . . uh," he almost gagged on the word, "gentleman wishes to speak with you." The man gave Longarm a dirty look and made a quick retreat into the safety of the kitchen.

"Yes?"

Kathleen Holcroft was as lovely as Longarm might have expected. She had that fine-boned, satin-complected elegance of appearance that only generations of gentle breeding can impart. No doubt she had been a beauty when she

54

was young. Moreover, she had that certain quality that would make her grow more attractive as she aged. Longarm found it impossible to guess how old she was now. She might have been anything from forty to fifty-five.

No wonder... Longarm forced that kind of idle speculation from his mind and put his thoughts back onto the task at hand.

"Sorry to bother you, ma'am, but I was looking to speak with your husband. The fella at the desk said him and his boys got in last night."

"That is correct, Mr. . . . ?"

"Custis, ma'am. Tom Custis."

"Do you have cattle you want Joseph to sell for you, Mr. Custis?"

"No, ma'am. But I need to get up Ogallala way, an' I understand your man drives cattle up there. I was hoping to hook on with his outfit, you see."

"Yes, I do see." The small amount of interest she had shown departed. She picked up the small pot and poured her cup full—tea, not coffee, Longarm noticed—and took a dainty sip from it. "Joseph's men have been with him for a long time. I doubt he would be interested in taking on strangers this late in the season. However, it is a matter you should take up with him directly. I never interfere in Joseph's business dealings."

"No, ma'am, I just thought . . ."

"They were quite late getting in last night. Joseph is still sleeping. I daresay he should be around this afternoon, though. You might look for him at the Longbranch. He tends to favor it when we are in Dodge."

Longarm glanced over his shoulder and lowered his voice to a level barely above a whisper. "There's places I'd rather not be seen, ma'am." That was certainly true enough, if not for the apparent reasons. "Could you ask him maybe to meet me somewhere else when he gets around?"

"I shall do no such thing." In spite of the refusal,

though, her voice was quite neutral. If she felt any disapproval, she failed to show it. Longarm could not decide if that was a matter of her breeding, or if she simply did not care that this stranger did not want to be recognized in town. And that, frankly, was one of the things about which he was extremely curious.

"If you still want to speak with Joseph," she continued, "I suggest you find your own method."

"Yes, ma'am."

"Good day." She turned her eyes back to the menu in front of her, dismissing him completely.

Longarm stood there for a moment longer, the Kossuth held before him, but he might as well have been invisible for all the attention Mrs. Holcroft paid. After a moment he turned and left the hotel. If he did not choose to go voluntarily, he was sure, the waiter would be most happy to call an officer and have him removed from the lady's presence.

Interesting, Longarm thought as he slipped through the alleys back toward the less respectable end of town. Damned interesting.

But he wished he had learned more than he had.

"Yes, thanks." Longarm accepted another thick slice of the roast beef he had brought back from town for Miss Crane to cook. Beef was readily available in Dodge, and he had carried back enough of it to last the household for several days.

He was pleased to see that Miss Crane seemed to have overcome her reluctance to eat heartily of the food he provided. She put another thick chunk of fat-rimmed roast on her plate also. Already he thought he could see an improvement in the young woman's color. Certainly there was improvement in the level of energy she displayed. If she kept on eating like this, both she and the babe would be fat and sassy in no time at all, he hoped.

"Could I ask you to do me a favor, Miss Crane?"

Her fork paused where it was, poised above a bit of

56

meat. She became motionless and, he thought, tense as well.

"I'd pay you, of course," he said.

Her eyes were lowered toward her plate, but he thought she might have blushed. "I couldn't accept money from you for . . . that, Mr. Custis. I simply couldn't. But I am in no position to deny you either." The fingers of one hand fumbled at her throat, and she was trembling.

Damn it, she had misunderstood him again. It embarrassed him, even though he was doing his best here to present himself as the kind of low son of a bitch who would think only of himself. But not with Miss Crane and the kid. Damn it, he hadn't done that under this roof.

"The favor is an errand, Miss Crane. Nothing else."

This time she definitely did blush. "I'm sorry, Mr. Custis."

"Yeah," he said. The bastard she'd been living with must have been a real winner to give her such an impression of men in general.

"Of course I will do you a favor. You don't have to pay me to run an errand," she told him.

"Thank you."

He had been thinking about this for much of the afternoon while he waited, hoping to find Joe Holcroft away from the dangers of Front Street.

Several times Longarm had seen the man from a distance. A poke at the stockyards had pointed Holcroft out to him. But the man never strayed from the neighborhood of the popular Longbranch and Alhambra. There were just too many other men in that vicinity whom Longarm also recognized, and who would certainly recognize him.

"Along about dark," Longarm said, "I'd like you to deliver a message to a gentleman. Ask him to meet me behind the stock pens."

Miss Crane glanced toward the baby lying in its makeshift bed in the corner. The infant was awake but content enough for the moment. It was carefully and repeatedly inspecting, and then tasting, one finger after another. The child seemed quite wrapped up in its investigations.

"You could carry him along or if you'd rather get someone to watch over him while you're away I could pay them something for that," Longarm suggested.

"After dark?" she asked.

"Yes." He thought he could see a faint, quickly concealed flicker of disapproval in her eyes. But she said nothing about that, whatever suspicions she may have harbored.

"That should give me time enough to clean up here then and to feed Pippin. Would that be all right?"

"Of course." Longarm finished his meal quickly and retreated behind the hanging blanket for a smoke and a pull at the bottle of Maryland rye while he waited for Miss Crane and for sundown.

Holcroft came. Longarm had watched from afar while Miss Crane asked for him first at the saloons and finally found him at the hotel.

The man did not come alone, though. Longarm saw him leave the hotel and separate from Miss Crane, the young woman hurrying back toward the river while Holcroft walked several blocks and disappeared inside one of the saloons on Front. When the drover came out again he had three men with him.

Cautious, Longarm thought. He wondered why Joe Holcroft thought he had to be so careful.

But perhaps it was only natural when a man was asked to meet a stranger in the darkness. Whatever the reason, Holcroft was taking no chances. The three men who accompanied him all moved with that sinuous, catlike grace that said they did not have to fear any company or any confrontation. These men were not, Longarm thought, typical trailhands.

"You wanted to see me?" Holcroft asked when they came near.

58

"Yes. Thanks for coming."

Holcroft shrugged. He reached into his pocket and produced two cigars, handing one to Longarm. He took out a match and struck it.

Fair enough, Longarm thought. Holcroft wanted a look at him, and there was no spill of lamplight this far away from Front. Longarm did not mind in the slightest, particularly since the cigar was as fine a leaf as he had ever tasted.

In exchange Holcroft gave Longarm a good look at himself when he used the same match to light his own cigar. Holcroft was a large man, healthy and trim despite the silver in his hair. Longarm guessed him to be in his fifties but still a vigorous and fit man. He had a prosperous, even distinguished bearing that would make him a fitting match for Kathleen. A truly handsome couple, Longarm thought.

"Now what is your business, Mr. . . . .?"

"Custis," Longarm told him. "Long Tom Custis."

"You'd be the man that was looking for me this morning, then. You spoke to my wife, I believe."

"That's right."

"I think she already told you that I'm not looking for hands."

"She didn't say that exactly. She said I'd have to ask you myself."

Holcroft shrugged. "She could have saved us both some trouble. I'm not looking for hands."

"I can handle cattle, Mr. Holcroft. And whatever else comes along."

"I'm not looking for hands," Holcroft repeated.

"I have to get to Ogallala."

"It's a free country. You're as welcome to go there as the next man. Perhaps I'll see you there." Holcroft turned and walked away.

The three men who had come with him to the rendezvous lagged behind for a bit, until Holcroft was well clear, before they turned and walked after him.

A hard crew, Longarm thought. Experienced. Careful without being the least bit nervous about it. And damned well competent.

He found it interesting, too, that none of them, not Holcroft or his silent watchdogs, seemed to find it at all unusual for someone to want to avoid being seen along Front Street. Definitely a hard crew. But why, if they were only the short-haul drovers they appeared to be?

It was an interesting question.

Longarm hooked his elbows on the top rail of the stock pen and propped the sole of his boot on the lowest rail. He nodded agreeably to Murphy, the cattle buyer, and offered the man a cheroot.

"Thankya." Murphy looked at him. "You're the fella was looking for Joe Holcroft the other day, aren't you?"

"Yes. Tom Custis."

"Of course. Sorry I didn't recall at first. You heard that Joe's back in town?"

"Yes, I did. Talked to him last night."

"Will you be consigning your herd with him, Tom? I don't mean to get personal with you, understand. But if you're looking for a buyer..."

Longarm never had exactly told Murphy why he wanted to talk with Joe Holcroft, so the assumption the man was making was a reasonable one.

"I appreciate your offer, Mr. Murphy. And in fact Mr. Holcroft won't be taking my herd. Fact is, I'm thinking of driving them on to Ogallala myself."

"I see." Murphy shifted the cheroot Longarm had given him to the other side of his jaw and nodded.

Longarm had been just talking. He hadn't actually planned what he was going to say until he heard it come out of his own mouth. But now that he thought about it, that wasn't a half-bad idea.

He had to find some logical excuse to keep an eye on Joe Holcroft and his crew.

Taking a small herd up the public droving road to Ogallala would certainly be reason enough.

And if he couldn't hire on with the Holcroft outfit perhaps they would let him throw his beeves in with theirs. There was always the excuse of being wary of Indian attack or herd-cutters or whatever.

Besides, the road was a public one. He would have as much right as anyone else to use it. Holcroft had said that himself.

By damn, he would do that. Take a little herd of cattle up the same trail, kind of like Murphy here had used that Judas steer the other night to put a load of beeves onto the boxcar.

It was sensible enough, Longarm thought. Hell, it might even work.

"I'm sorry," Longarm said. "I didn't catch that." Murphy had been saying something while Longarm was wool-gathering about the idea of using a Judas herd to keep track of Holcroft and his crowd.

"I said I don't know that I'd take the chance if I were you, Tom." The buyer smiled. "Of course I have to admit that I've a prejudiced view on the subject, but I really don't think you'll make out on the move. Not when you have to pay wages to your hands and gamble on the higher pay-out in Ogallala."

"What was the difference this morning, Mr. Murphy?" Not that Longarm really cared what the difference was or indeed if there was one at all. He asked the question only for the sake of form.

"A dollar a head," Murphy admitted. "But I'll tell you quite honestly, Mr. Custis, that my packer in Kansas City has already advised me to expect a drop in price before the end of the week. If Kansas City reduces price, Chicago is almost certain to follow suit."

"To a level as low as the Kansas City market?"

Murphy shook his head. "I shouldn't think so. After all, the Kansas City market is fed from the southern herds.

Texas, leases in the Indian Territories, some coming all the way over from New Mexico. All those are loaded with beef. The situation up north is different. Plenty of unappropriated lands up that way, all through Nebraska and Wyoming and on up into the Dakota country and Montana. Ranchers up that way are still concentrating on stocking their land and appropriating more grass for themselves, so there are fewer cattle coming onto the market up there. That's why the Chicago packers are having to pay more for their beef.

"I don't believe that will hold for too many more years, mind you. As the land is taken up and fully stocked there will be more animals sold off. When that happens the prices in Chicago and Kansas City should even out. For the time being, though, I think you can reasonably expect to get more from the Chicago packers."

Murphy frowned and took a puff on the cheroot. "I don't want you to think, Mr. Custis, that I'm just giving you a pitch so I can buy your herd. I'm interested in buying from you, I admit that. But I would not be willing to mislead you for that purpose."

"I understand that, Mr. Murphy."

"Well, what I want to warn you about is that once the Kansas City price falls, as I fully expect it to, the Chicago packers will see that as an opportunity to reduce their costs also. They should remain fifty cents, even a dollar higher than the Kansas City price. But if the Kansas City offering is a dollar off from what it is today—and that is what my packer leads me to believe—you might very well make that drive north and pay your hands their wages for an additional two or three weeks and yet end up selling your herd at the very same price that I could offer you today."

"But it might not work that way?" Longarm asked.

"Absolutely," Murphy agreed. "I own no crystal balls, Tom." He smiled. "If I did, I would be a rich man today. And I don't mean to discourage you. I just want you to understand the things that may, or as easily may *not*, happen in the market during the next few weeks."

"I appreciate that, Mr. Murphy. But then, like the man says, if you don't pay the ante you can't win the pot. I think I'll take the gamble."

"I wish you luck, Tom, I truly do."

"Thank you, Mr. Murphy."

Longarm turned away from the pens, crowded as always with bawling, horn-clacking beeves making the long journey from the cactus-studded grazing lands of Texas to the dining rooms and kitchens of a hungry East.

Yeah, Longarm told himself. That wasn't a half-bad idea. He could take his own herd north and use that as an excuse to stay within spying distance of Joe Holcroft and his men. It should work.

Longarm grinned wryly to himself. Now all he needed was a herd of longhorn cattle and a crew to drive them for him.

Chapter 7

"Are you out of your mind, Deputy?" The blue-coat was red-faced and irritable. That was all right, but now he was becoming loud as well.

"I'd appreciate it if you'd keep your voice down, Colonel. No one is supposed to know I'm here." Longarm tipped his chair back against the wall and crossed his legs, raking his shin with those damned Mexican spurs when he did so. He would have thought he would have adjusted to the things by now, but he hadn't. He reached into a pocket for a cheroot and lit it without offering one to the florid post commander.

"And I would appreciate it, sir, if you would be reasonable."

"I've already explained the problem to you, Colonel. I need a herd of cattle. You have a bunch of them waiting for delivery at the reservations. All I want to do is borrow some of them for a spell."

"But—"

"Really, colonel, you've read the regs just as closely as I have. The Justice Department is authorized to draw on War Department livestock for line-of-duty requirements. And what I require, Colonel, is a herd of bovines. Not so big a herd. Just five hundred head or so." Longarm put the end of the cheroot into the corner of his jaw and tried to look sympathetic. Colonel Markham was new at Fort Dodge, only on the job for a month or so. In point of fact, Longarm did feel rather sympathetic toward him. Markham was not all that old a man, but assignment to Dodge meant that he was being put out to pasture. He would likely stay here until he died.

There had been a time, a brief time, when Fort Dodge was an action post, an important part of the chain of forts with the mission of protecting the Santa Fe Trail trade. Now, with the rails already west of Dodge and the Trail dying if not quite yet dead, Fort Dodge was as ailing as this eastern end of the Trail.

Now the only function of the two under-strength infantry companies here was to serve as a buying point for beef destined for tribal annuity payments. And perhaps as a place to warehouse soldiers too old, too unstable, or simply too troublesome to be wanted anywhere else. The quality of personnel Longarm had seen in and around the post was not the highest, and Colonel Markham would certainly be sensitive to all that that meant.

So the poor man really had more troubles than a late-night visit from a deputy United States marshal.

"Damn it, man, that regulation refers to transportation needs. It has to do with drawing a horse or a wagon. If you need a horse—"

"I told you what I need, Colonel. And I don't believe the regulations specify transportation. What it says is livestock, regardless of what it might have intended."

Markham glared down at the battered cover of the book of standing orders and War Department regulations that lay closed on his desk. He had just finished re-reading the appropriate section. So had Longarm. "We both know what it intended," Markham grumbled.

"We both know what it says, too."

"I'm not even sure that those cattle belong to the War Department, Deputy. They really belong to the Bureau of Indian Affairs. That's Department of the Interior, not War."

"No, sir," Longarm said stubbornly. "I think you'll find that in the book too. The War Department, specifically the army, is required to procure and control annuity beeves until they are delivered to a reservation agent. Now let me get this right, Colonel." Longarm tilted his head back and closed his eyes as if in concentration. The truth was that he had never had occasion to care what those regulations said and was making up the wording from whole cloth.

"If I remember correctly, Colonel, the directive says you are to deliver such livestock to a reservation agent or to other such duly authorized representatives of the United States government as shall be deemed appropriate. In this case, sir, a duly authorized representative of the Justice Department. Simple." He smiled. "It's all right there in the regulations."

Markham fingered the loose-leaf book for a moment. Long enough that Longarm began to worry that the man might actually insist on reading the fantasy directive for himself. Then he frowned and Longarm knew he was home free.

"Five hundred head?" Markham asked.

"I could make do with four hundred if that would be better for you." It was time to give a little.

"I might be able to let you have four hundred head. But you must sign for them."

"Of course."

"Damned inconvenient," the colonel complained.

"Yes, sir." Longarm stood and reached for his hat. "One other thing, sir."

"What now, Deputy?"

"I can't let anyone see that I'm getting these critters from the army. So we'll have to arrange a delivery off away from the fort. And it'd be a good idea if you could send your herders out in civilian clothes when I pick them up."

"You expect me to ask my men—"

"Naturally," Longarm went on, as if he had not heard the beginnings of the outburst, "naturally I'll put in my own report to Washington an account of your cooperation and assistance on this case, sir."

Markham's frown softened a little. A man in a hopelessly career-ending position like Markham's could almost be counted on to grasp at straws.

As for the promised report to Washington, hell, all manner of superfluous paperwork was apt to wind up there eventually. Including that from the Denver office held down—at least for the moment—by Billy Vail. So Longarm did not feel that he had lied, exactly.

"I really do appreciate your assistance, sir," he said.

Markham grunted unhappily, but for the first time since this conversation had begun he looked at least a little bit pleased. Longarm had given the man some slight measure of hope, and that should count for something.

"Thank you, sir. I'll get in touch with you to work out the details of the transfer."

"Yes, well . . . yes," said Markham.

The kid had guts. Longarm had to give him that much. He had guts but not much else, no matter how rough-and-tough he tried to walk, talk, dress, and act.

His clothes could have come straight out of a *Harper's Weekly* illustration, sombrero, fringed shirt, and all. He was even trying to grow a moustache, but was several years short of being able to accomplish it. A pair of empty holsters on his hips showed that he hadn't much experience carrying steel while trying to ride a rank horse. Right now a hammer-headed yellow horse was dancing a jig on top of the fallen firearms, and if the kid lost his grip on the horn that same animal looked perfectly willing to stomp on the boy too.

Longarm hooked an elbow over the top rail of the livery-stable pen and joined the crowd of cowboys who were having their morning's amusement at the youngster's expense. This sort of excitement would not have been welcomed over by the stockyards, where the idea was to keep the cattle quiet, but here a boy in store-fresh jeans and a funny-looking shirt was fair game.

At least the kid had a little sense to go with his determination. The real trailhands talked big about never having to grab for the horn, but there wasn't a one of them that wouldn't do the same as this kid when the choice was between hanging on or losing the horse.

The boy was holding tick-tight with hands, legs, and spurs, and Longarm didn't doubt that he would have taken a pull with his teeth, too, if he'd had the chance of it.

The yellow horse pitched and squealed and tried its damnedest to unload the rider.

On top of the critter the kid looked pretty pale. His head was snapping back and forth like the popper on a bull-whacker's whip every time the horse changed direction, and there was a trickle of blood from his nose from where the yellow horse had butted him in the face with the back of its own shaggy head.

Around three sides of the pen hooting, yelling cowboys called out encouragement—to the horse, not the kid. There wasn't much doubt about where most of the money had been put in this contest.

The horse lunged forward with a loud grunt of effort, leaped high, and came down into a bone-jarring halt with all four legs braced rigid. The kid was caught leaning and was flung forward, doubled over with his nose in the yellow mane and the saddlehorn pushed deep into his gut. There was pain on the kid's face, and he was bleeding heavily now and gulping for air through a slack-jawed open

69

mouth. The cowboys around the pen began to hoot all the louder.

The kid lost his grip on the reins, and now the yellow horse had its head free and could really go to work. A sensible man would have cut his losses right there and jumped free, but the kid continued to hang on.

The infuriated horse let out a trumpet call of rage and threw itself backward. All the way back, past the last possible point of balance. Either the kid didn't know to jump or he was too scared to let go. The horse flipped over, taking both of them to the ground and rolling quickly free. It was only plain dumb luck that kept the kid from being speared by the saddlehorn.

The horse staggered back onto its feet, shook itself like a dog coming out of a creek, and blew a spray of snot as it cleared the dust from its nostrils. Then, apparently perfectly calm, the horse wandered over to an empty feed trough and began to nuzzle into the corners for stray bits of grain.

The kid lay sprawled out on the ground, out of breath and filthy with dust and blood and dried manure. He looked like he hadn't decided yet if he was hurt or not. After a while he sat up and shook himself, very much the way the horse had done. He was too weak to stand upright, though. He had to crawl on hands and knees to the fence rails and pull himself up hand over hand to get back onto his feet.

"You all right, son?" Longarm asked softly. The kid was practically face to face with him inside the pen but looked unaware of anything outside the confines of the rails.

"Hell, yes," the kid mumbled. He turned and began to stagger toward the yellow horse again. "Whoa, you son of a bitch. Whoa."

The horse flicked one ear back and sidled away from him. The kid stumbled after it. It was clear, though, that he would not be able to catch the animal. He would be lucky to negotiate the width of the corral without falling flat on his face.

"What's the deal?" Longarm asked the man next to him.

"Twenty to ten the horse can't be rode." The cowboy grinned. "Easy money."

The kid stumbled and went to one knee. Longarm bent to duck through the rails and helped the kid onto his feet. "Are you all right?" he asked again.

The kid tried to shake his arm free of Longarm's grip, heading for the yellow horse still.

"You have ten dollars on this," Longarm said. "Can you afford to lose it?"

The kid looked at him for the first time. He ran the back of his hand under his dripping nose, making blood-colored mud in the dirt that coated him. "What d'you think?"

Longarm grinned at him. "Can you ride the horse?"

"I'll ride the sumbitch."

"All right." Longarm looked toward the ring of men who were enjoying the view from the comfortable side of the rails. "I'm adding twenty to the kid's bet," he called loudly. "Any takers?" The response was a human stampede toward a tall, wind-weathered ranny who seemed to have taken charge of the wagering.

"Ride him, then," Longarm told the kid.

Longarm approached the horse and grabbed its reins. He held the yellow animal steady while the kid climbed hand over hand into the saddle. The boy looked wrung out and ready to die, but he was hell for stubborn and obviously didn't know that he was whipped. He accepted the reins, took a deep seat, and shoved his brand-new boots deep into the stirrups. That could lead to a dragging if he came off the horse, but was more secure. Obviously the kid did not intend to come off a second time. He nodded, and Longarm let go of the cheekstrap he'd been holding.

The yellow horse began to tremble. Its sweat-lathered skin rippled, and its muscles tensed.

Then the big horse went crazy.

Chapter 8

Longarm poured Maryland rye into two glasses and shoved one in front of the kid. The boy was shaking so badly, probably from a combination of exhaustion and the after-effects of fear, that he had to steady one hand with the other in order to get the glass to his lips. He drained the liquor off in one gulp and shuddered. Longarm poured him another.

"Feeling better?"

The kid nodded.

"I got to give you credit, son. I never thought you could ride him. No one thought you could get back up that last time."

The boy grinned past lips that were puffy and swollen. His whole face looked like someone had had at him with a meat tenderizer, and he was dripping wet from washing off. But he looked pleased. He took a smaller swallow of the rye this time.

"I learned back home you can't outmuscle a horse," the kid said. "Just outstubborn them."

"Where's home?"

The kid hesitated a moment, then shrugged. "Rhode Island. An' if you wanta laugh, go ahead. I ain't ashamed of where I'm from."

"No need to be. What's your name, son?"

"William Henry Harrison Jones." He said it proudly. "What's yours?"

"Tom Custis. Some call me Long Tom."

"Most call me Willie."

"All right, Willie. I'm proud to know you."

"Same here, Mr. Custis."

"Tom," Longarm corrected.

"I'd shake your hand, Tom, except I'd rather not have it squoze right now." He grinned and finished off the rye.

Longarm poured for both of them again. "Are you looking for work, Willie?"

"Yes, sir. But I ain't looking for no damn charity. I got me twenty dollars. That'll last a while if need be."

"I said work; I meant work. I need some help driving a small herd of cattle up the Ogallala Trail."

Willie's eyes got big and his grin got bigger. "Really? A real cow drive?"

"Uh-uh. Low pay, no sleep, and all the dust you can eat. That's about what a real drive is. Are you interested?"

"Interested? Hell, Mr. Custis . . . I mean Tom . . . I'd pay you that twenty dollars just to let me come along on a real cow drive. That's what I came out here hoping to do. But I got to be honest with you. I'm no cowhand. I never been a cowboy before. But I sure Lord always wanted to be one." His eyes were bright with excitement.

"You can ride, and you have grit. If you want the job it's yours."

"I do," Willie said with feeling.

"Then you're hired." Longarm took a sip from his glass and thought for a moment. He did not really expect danger

74

on the trail. Mostly he just wanted to be able to stay within eyeball distance of Holcroft and his herd. And young men like Willie Jones, inexperienced on the trail and with no preconceptions about what to expect next, would be unlikely to ask questions if the boss did not tend to business the way a more experienced trailhand would expect. "Tell me, Willie. Are there any other young men like you in town looking for their first drive?"

"Yes, sir." Willie made a face. "Though I got to admit we weren't so damn bright coming to Dodge City. Except it's always Dodge you hear about an' read about back home. I guess I never thought of it much, but this here is where the drives end up. A fella as wants a job, he's got to be where the drives start, not where they end. But I hadn't thought of that before I left home, and I guess the other fellas didn't neither. But I sure ain't the only one in town."

"I need to hire three good men, Willie. You're the first of them. Do you think you could find me two more with as much grit as you've got?"

"Easy. I could get you a dozen if you could use 'em."

"Just two more will do."

"It's as good as done, Tom."

"Do you have your own saddles?"

Willie's face fell.

"That's all right," Longarm assured him quickly. "I'll provide horses and gear." Although how he was going to do that... The fort would only be able to provide horses with Remount Service brands and issue saddles, so that was out. He would just have to think of something. If nothing else, he could put through a voucher for cash and buy them. That was one good point about Dodge. Trail-wise horses were always available and always cheap, being sold off by crews that did not want the bother of driving a remuda home with them. And used saddles were equally available, trade-ins left behind by cowboys who had blown a part of their trail wages on fancy new rigs that would catch the young ladies' attention.

Longarm grunted quietly to himself. He would work it out, one way or another. The thing now was to get it done. Rumor had it that with the price of beef on a downslide, herd owners were practically lined up and ready to fight for the privilege of having Joe Holcroft take their beeves on to Ogallala with the promise of greater profits there.

If the rumors were true, Holcroft would be able to drive as many cattle north as his crew could handle.

"I'm sure glad I ran into you, Tom."

"My pleasure, Willie. Another drink?"

"No, sir." The kid grinned. "I got to go line up the rest of our crew now."

"You just do that, Willie. I'll see you later tonight. We can meet here."

"You bet, boss."

"Tom," Longarm corrected. But he was already speaking to the boy's back. Willie was already rushing off, his beating by the yellow horse forgotten in the excitement of getting his first real cow-driving job.

Longarm watched him go and tried to decide if he should envy the kid that eagerness of youth or feel sorry for him because of it.

The simple truth was that Longarm really didn't know.

His arms were more than a little tired by the time he got down to the shack where he was boarding. Longarm did not expect to be in Dodge very much longer. Whenever Holcroft pulled out, he and his boys would have to be right behind. When he left, he wanted to leave Anne Crane and her child well stocked with food, so he was carrying quite an armload with him.

"Hello," he said cheerfully as he pushed his way through the canvas drape over the door.

Miss Crane was nursing the baby, one milk-swollen breast exposed with the infant sucking noisily. Her other nipple had leaked a bit, causing a dark stain on the front of her dress. Longarm pretended not to notice. He turned his

76

back on the young mother and set the heavy box of food down on the table. "I brought some more fixings," he said unnecessarily.

"Shh."

"Ma'am?" He turned. She was arranging a diaper over herself and the babe. Longarm thought she looked nervous. He hoped she didn't think . . .

"Shh," she repeated. She pointed anxiously toward the blanket that curtained his sleeping quarters off from the rest of the room.

From behind it, now that he was paying attention, Longarm could hear the deep, slow breathing of someone asleep. "Don't wake him. Whatever you do, Mr. Custis, please don't wake him," Miss Crane whispered. She wasn't just nervous, she was afraid.

"Who?" he whispered back at her.

"James."

James. That was the child's name. But he sure wasn't asleep. He was right there under the cloth going hard at his dinner. For a moment Longarm failed to understand. Then he realized the child would have been named for his father. "Your, uh . . . friend?"

Miss Crane blushed. She also nodded.

In a normal voice this time, he asked, "Do you want me to throw him out of here?"

"No!" she said quickly. She still looked frightened.

"I don't mean to butt in, ma'am, but the way you were talking before . . . well, you don't have to put up with anything you don't want. I could see to that."

"No," she said again. She bit at her lower lip and lowered her eyes from him.

If that was the way it was, Longarm thought, if she was still in love with the son of a bitch and wanted to take him back in now, it wasn't any of his business. The only thing he could do about it would be to move quietly along.

He thought fleetingly about the food he had brought into the house. So, screw James. Longarm had brought the things for the needy woman and her child. He wasn't going to do them dirty just because of some bastard he'd never so much as met. "I have some things in there. Should I get them or do you want to?"

"I . . . you better let me do it." She stood and the diaper slipped off her shoulder. Her breasts, he noticed, were very pale and blue-veined, her skin quite thin and lightly freckled. The baby had drifted off to sleep with his mother's nipple still in his tiny mouth.

Longarm turned his head away and fumbled uselessly in the box of foodstuffs.

He heard Miss Crane enter the partitioned sleeping area. A moment later there was a change in the rhythm of James's breathing, then a loud snort and a creak of protest from the rope-sprung cot.

"Where the fuck d'you think you're goin' with that?"

"The boarder, the gentleman I told you about? He's moving out. He needs his things."

"Gentleman, my ass," James protested. "Some saddle-tramp son of a bitch you took up with the minute my back was turned. That's more like it." There was a loud, moist sound as James hawked phlegm into his throat and spat on the floor. "Tell the bastard he's out o' luck, Annie. You're mine an' so is whatever he left here."

Longarm stepped behind the blanket and removed his hat, bowing politely in Miss Crane's direction. "Would you excuse us for a few minutes, miss?" He smiled at her. She looked paler than ever and very frightened.

James, propped on one elbow in Longarm's rumpled bed, scowled. He probably thought he was looking ferocious.

The man was big, no question about that. Dark, greasy hair spilled down over his forehead and matted his chest with tight curls. Longarm was not sure if he was growing a beard or was just long overdue for a shave.

"Mr. Custis . . ." Miss Crane's fear must have infected the child, because Pippin woke up and began to cry.

"James and I want to talk," Longarm said calmly. "Excuse us. Please?"

"Talk!" James growled. "That'll be the fuckin' day."

"One of the things we need to talk about is your choice of language in the presence of a lady," Longarm said. His voice was deceptively mild, although anyone with any scrap of perception could have detected the chill that lay underneath it.

James apparently lacked that sensitivity. The man laughed and swept the sheet back. He was wearing drawers but nothing else. His legs were as hairy as the rest of him. "Little ol' Annie here is private property, mister. I talk how I damn well please in front of her. An' if you wanta tell me otherwise, asshole, I'll break your fuckin' neck for you. Now get out of here. Annie, cook me somethin' to eat. An' get that kid shut. I'm horny, an' I don't wanta listen to the kid bawl while we have our fun." He was speaking to the woman, but he continued to look at Longarm, grinning, taunting him with his power over Anne Crane.

"Please, Miss Crane," Longarm said. "Take the child outside."

She looked helplessly from James to Longarm and back again. "Get your ass outa here," James barked. "I told you to cook, didn't I? So go find somethin' to cook."

Miss Crane turned and fled, out of the little bedroom area and on out of the shack. Longarm waited until he was sure she was well out of hearing before he spoke again.

"You made a mistake, James. You pissed me off. I mean you *really* pissed me off."

James snorted his lack of concern about that. He stood and reached for his trousers.

Instead of putting them on, though, he dropped them onto the floor. When he turned to face Longarm he had an oversized knife in his fist.

"Scare a lot of pilgrims with that thing, do you?" Longarm asked. "I've never liked them all that much myself. Not stout enough for serious fighting."

James paused and blinked several times in rapid succession. This affair was not going the way it was supposed to. This Custis fellow didn't look scared.

"But I thank you," Longarm said. "Now that you've pulled steel on me, I don't have to feel sorry about what happens next."

"You won't be able to feel sorry, mister. You won't be able to feel nothing at all."

A blusterer, Longarm thought, and a bully too. He wondered how the woman had ever come to the conclusion that this pathetic son of a bitch was worth anything. Why would a girl like Anne Crane have taken up with him in the first place? But then, it was hardly a revelation that taste was a damned personal sort of thing, and something no one person could decide for another.

Longarm stood relaxed, his weight on his left boot, and waited for James to work himself up to it.

James scowled some more, spat on the floor, went into his very best imitation of a knife-fighter's crouch, and made some semi-fancy feints and passes with the gleaming blade of the knife. Longarm supposed he ought to be frightened as all billy-hell of the performance, but somehow he couldn't quite work up to it. James looked a whole lot better than he was. All style but no substance.

James finally got tired of waiting for Longarm to keel over in a faint. He scuttled forward, knife held low, balanced quite properly in his palm with the blade extended and the cutting edge upward. Maybe he had actually used the thing a time or two, Longarm conceded. But if he had it likely had been against other knife men. Or cowboys. Cowboys despised—and generally were damn well scared of—knives. If it couldn't be handled with a gun they didn't want to mess with it, generally. Old James had probably taken advantage of that fact too easily in the past.

Longarm let him come closer, waiting.

As James came in range his left hand darted up to draw

his opponent's attention while the right hand holding the knife swept in a quick, vicious arc that was intended to disembowel.

Most men facing that threat would have jumped back out of reach of the blade, off balance but for the moment safe.

A very few more knowledgable fighters would have stepped forward, inside the sweep of the knife to grapple.

Longarm stood where he was. The edge of his left hand flashed down, chopping at James's wrist.

At the same time, his weight already poised, he jerked his knee up and lashed forward with the toe of his pointed boot.

The boot slashed into James's crotch, and James let out a howl of pain that tailed off into a low, moaning bleat as he dropped to the floor. Longarm noticed, though, that he still had the knife. It had not fallen.

Longarm stepped around behind him, wary of the threat of a backhanded slash with the blade.

"It isn't that I don't trust you," Longarm said, "but let's be sure about this."

Longarm delivered another kick to the point of the man's spine. James straightened and screamed. This time he lost his hold on the knife. The thing went skittering across the floor.

"Thank you." Longarm went around the quivering man and picked up the knife. It was no better made than others like it he had seen. Decent enough manufacture but an inherently weak design. He laid the blade over the toe of one boot with the haft propped on the floor and with the sole of his other boot stepped down on the section where the blade and handle joined. The knife broke in two with a sharp snap, and he kicked the separate pieces under the bed.

James, still in agony on the floor, had murder in his eyes.

"You aren't convinced, are you?" Longarm asked. He walked toward James. The big man was sweating now. "I'm gonna kill you."

"I don't think so."

James lunged awkwardly, strong hands groping for a hold, any hold, that would enable him to close with this man, and to crush him.

Longarm kicked James in the face. The big man's head snapped back, and blood flew, but still the man tried to claw his way forward. The man could be as dangerous as he was mean.

Longarm felt no regrets at all, no hesitation. He side-stepped the next sprawling lunge, bent and twisted with James's wrist clamped in Longarm's hands.

He straightened the arm and twisted again, locking the elbow joint into rigid immobility.

Deliberately, just as he had done with the joint between knife blade and handle, Longarm positioned the sole of his boot and applied quick, hard pressure.

The elbow gave with a loud, rather dull snap, and James screamed.

Longarm let go of that wrist and reached for the other. James was going to be out of the bully business for a very long time. The big man screamed again and then collapsed in a dead faint. His complexion was pasty pale, and his whole body was covered with sudden sweat. The pain must have been excruciating.

Longarm picked up his saddlebags and stepped outside. Anne Crane and the baby were watching from a few yards away. The woman looked as pale as when Longarm had first seen her and seemed not even to notice the baby that was howling in her arms.

When she saw which of the men came outside un-scathed she let out a sharp yelp of dismay and began to run toward the shack where her man lay injured.

She gave Longarm a glance as she raced past that was every bit as murderous as James's had been.

"Well, I'll be damned," Longarm muttered to himself. Apparently Miss Crane hadn't *wanted* to be rescued from the hairy son of a bitch.

No, Longarm told himself as he walked toward the shed where the horse was tied, there wasn't much accounting for taste . . . or judgment.

He saddled Tom Bradley's good horse, lashed his saddlebags in place behind the cantle, and got the hell out of there. It looked like he would have to find some other place to spend the night tonight.

Chapter 9

"Mr. Custis, I'd like you t'meet Roy Garrett—Roy's the tall one there—and Harvey Moelken. Roy an' Harvey, they'll do for you just as hard and honest as I will, Mr. Custis. You got my personal word on it." Willie looked proud and puffed up and perhaps just a bit self-important before his friends, too, as he introduced them to their new boss.

Longarm grunted and shook hands with both of the youngsters. Garrett was by far the bigger of the two, standing a head taller than Moelken, very nearly as tall as Longarm. He seemed shy at first meeting, but there was a quiet air of competence about him, too, although he was dressed in overalls and a homespun shirt. He looked like he had come straight off an East Texas cotton farm. Longarm wondered if he was any kin to Pat Garrett of New Mexico. There was enough physical resemblance, in the breadth of his shoulders, the set of his jaw, the shape of his nose, to raise the question, but Longarm did not ask it aloud. Longarm knew Pat well enough from past encounters and did not want to get into any discussions about long-lost relatives.

Moelken, in contrast, was a short, slender banty rooster not yet out of his teens. He was pale enough that if he had been a few years older Longarm would have wondered if he had been spending his recent time behind steel bars. More likely he was the product of some small-town shopkeeper's stock room.

Both young men carried cheap, elderly revolvers prominent on their belts, although unlike William Henry Harrison Jones they had paid for one apiece.

Looking at them, Longarm could not help but be amused. All three of them were bound and determined to dress the part of rough, tough cowboys, just like in the illustrations back East. Longarm found that amusing, but they themselves were serious as hell about it. They'd gone off in search of adventure, by golly they'd found it. Good for them, Longarm thought.

"You fellows just do what you're told," Longarm said after the pleasantries were over, "and we'll all get along fine. I won't ask more of you than you can give. Nor any less. The pay is twenty dollars a month and found. For that I'll expect you to work all the day long and half the night as well. Longer if need be. If that doesn't satisfy you, speak up now."

The response from all three of them was a set of wide, wide grins.

They had a job, by damn, driving cattle up the Ogallala Trail. Not satisfied? Longarm strongly suspected that they would have paid him for the privilege of working day and night if only they'd had any money. Willie had said as much.

"Those saddles on the ground over there are yours. Yours to keep when we get to Ogallala." The grins got even wider. "If you stick, that is, but I expect you to. They aren't much, but they'll do. Take your pick. By the saddles you'll find some flour sacks. I didn't lay out for saddlebags for you, so use those to tie your personal things behind your cantles. And the first thing I want to see going into those sacks is your hardware." The grins commenced to fade. Not much, but a little.

"I don't know what you've heard or seen or read," Longarm went on as if he hadn't noticed, "but on most good crews there are rules against guns. They aren't of much use around cattle except for causing stampedes and making trouble. There are rules against drinking and gambling too.

"Soon as you sort out what saddle belongs to who and get your gear ready we'll pick out some horses. That's our remuda in the pen over there. Only two head apiece, since we aren't going far and we sure as hell aren't going fast. We'll each have a day horse and a night horse." The grins expanded again.

"The man riding drag will be responsible for bringing the spare mounts behind on a long string. Them and the pack mule. I'll mostly be riding point, but you men will take turns on the flanks and pulling drag. We all ride night-hawk. Harvey will pair off with me for the second shift each night. Roy will ride with you, Willie. And, Willie, you'll be my segundo on the drive. When I'm not handy the decisions fall to you.No extra pay for that. Just extra work. All right?"

It was definitely all right.

"Good enough," Longarm told them. "Get to it, then. We pick up the cattle this afternoon and hold them on the grass north of town until I decide they're ready to trail together." Which would be, although he did not mention it, right at the same time Joe Holcroft pulled out with his herd.

"Any questions?"

"No, sir."

"Nope."

"Not me."

"Then go pick out your saddles," he told them.

Longarm had seen stampedes that were slower and less noisy than the rush to examine the beat-up saddles Longarm had found for them. It was like Christmas morning in a rich man's house, at least the way they acted over it.

Longarm found himself grinning toward their backsides as the three youngsters—the oldest of them probably wasn't more than eighteen—bent down to exclaim over the battered gear and to match pennies for who got first pick.

Longarm finished smothering the breakfast fire with a final kick of dirt. "Saddle up," he told them. "We move the herd this morning."

"Really?" They looked eager after three days of close-herding the cattle north of Dodge City.

"Yup. They're ready."

The truth was that the cattle had been ready for the trail from the minute Longarm and the boys had picked them up from the civilian-clothed soldiers. Three hundred eighty-five head of rangy, spotted beeves. The sergeant in charge of the detail hadn't known any reason for the odd number, but at least the receipt Longarm signed for them was correct.

The youngsters hurried to their day horses and began the rather slow and inexperienced process of saddling them. Roy Garrett, Longarm noticed, still held back, taking his time and pretending an interest in a twist of tobacco so that he could watch Willie and Harvey and mimic their actions. Roy obviously didn't know a crupper from a crapper yet, but he was learning.

Longarm knew better than to ask any of them to build the packs that would carry their food and few utensils. He did that himself rather than risk a sore-backed mule. But he saw them watching him closely while trying to give the

88

appearance that they were not. That, too, they would learn before the drive was over.

"The way this works," Longarm said, "is that we go slow and easy. This isn't a race, and we don't want to run the fat off them. That would cost money when we go to sell them in Ogallala. You understand?"

The boys nodded dutifully, whether they understood or not. And whether they did or not really didn't matter. What mattered was that they were willing to follow Longarm's instructions.

"Since we have such a small herd to manage, and since cattle by nature are more comfortable with other cows around, I may even decide to follow another herd, to keep the cattle and us out of trouble." He reinforced the lie with a smile. These inexperienced youngsters wouldn't know what was normal on a drive, that a small herd would travel together just as easily—more so, even—than a large one. Or especially that it was a damnfool move for one herd to follow close on the heels of another, simply because the first herd would be getting the good grazing and the cattle moving behind would be bound to lose weight and value because of that. He certainly wasn't likely to mention to them that his real interest on the drive was to keep an eye on Joe Holcroft and his men.

"We'll move them out slow," Longarm said. "You probably expect them to move in a tight bunch, like they are when they bed for the night, but they'll string out. Once we get them moving, they'll come along almost single file. Even a herd this size will thin out to a line a quarter of a mile or longer when they're on the move. It's natural, so don't worry about it and don't try to force them to go against their nature. We mostly just keep 'em calm and keep 'em moving. Any questions?"

"No." They probably had plenty, but were too embarrassed to show their ignorance.

"Then let's move them." Longarm swung into the saddle of the tough little cowpony he had bought in Dodge and led the way to the just-waking herd. Tom Bradley's much better mount was reserved for the important night duty when a man's life might well depend on the sense of his horse. With a minimum of fuss and noise, Longarm got the herd leaders pointed west and slowly moving. Willie took the south flank and Harvey the north. Roy brought up the rear, leading the mule and horses in the drag.

By late morning Longarm was becoming worried. There was no sign of the Holcroft herd, although the word was that they were to have moved out in the pre-dawn.

Then, off to his right, he saw the low haze that would almost have to be the dust raised by their movement. Apparently Holcroft was hanging well north of the Arkansas River, except probably for watering several times a day.

That was reasonable, Longarm decided. Holcroft and his men had taken other herds up this trail several times during the summer. The grass close to the river would probably be short, with little time for recovery between the brief drives. So it was only good husbandry to vary the route somewhat.

Longarm increased the speed of his own drive slightly and delayed the noon stop—made for the benefit of the cattle, so the bovines could graze undisturbed for a while at midday—until he got a good look at Holcroft's herd.

He was damn near awed when he finally saw it.

The herd went on for miles. Literally, it covered a distance of several miles. That was one hell of a lot of cows, even accounting for the fact that a trail herd had no great density at any given point.

Willie rode up beside Longarm. The wind had been coming down from the north, and Willie was layered with dust from riding on the south flank of their own tiny herd. The kid stood in his stirrups to get a better look at the huge expanse of cow-dotted grass before them. "Jesus. Is that every critter in Kansas strung out over there?"

"Looks like it, doesn't it?"

"Yes, sir, it sure does. How many. . .?"

"I'm not sure exactly. A normal trail herd is something like three thousand head. My guess would be . . . I don't know . . . maybe close to twice that out there, all in that one herd. Five thousand head, anyway."

"Jesus," Willie repeated.

"Yeah."

Willie was disbelieving. So was Longarm, if for different reasons.

William Henry Harrison Jones simply had never seen so damn many cattle in one place at one time unless it was in a stockyard, and the close confinement of a yard would make such a herd much less impressive to view.

Longarm's reasoning was quite different. Why the hell had Holcroft agreed to take on so many cattle for this drive?

The man hadn't increased the size of his crew. Longarm knew that for a fact from his quiet conversations around Dodge during the past few days.

The man had a crew perfectly suited to handle three thousand head on the trail, but not five. Another two thousand head should have meant at least another five or six men to handle them properly.

Holcroft had hired no such extra hands.

There was no way any sensible drover could expect to handle so many extra beeves without risk of loss. Yet Holcroft had expressed no interest in the scores of out-of-work trail-end hands who were available in the town.

Yet the man had given written guarantees of dollar-per-head increases when the beeves were sold in Ogallala, with no deductions for loss, theft, or deaths en route from Dodge to Nebraska.

That alone was suspicious as hell. Yet the few owners Longarm had been able to talk to about it said that Joe Holcroft's record was sound. Ever since the first herds began to arrive in Dodge during the spring, Holcroft had been moving consignment herds north to Ogallala and returning solid profits to the owners.

They had been small herds to begin with. One man Longarm spoke with over drinks in Dodge said he himself had consigned only two hundred head to Holcroft that spring. Now, back with a second herd before fall's loss of good graze between Texas and Kansas put an end to the droving season for this year, the man was practically begging Holcroft to take on a sizeable number of beeves on his behalf.

Longarm grunted to himself and reached for a cheroot while he continued to study the huge herd sprawled out before him. Maybe it was just that simple. Maybe so many owners had pressed their cattle on Holcroft that the man had caved in to the pressure and agreed to take on more than he could reasonably handle.

Still, it made a fellow wonder.

"We'll stop the leaders now," Longarm said to Willie, turning his attention back to his own little bunch, "and let the others drift in at their own pace. Let 'em graze a bit while we eat. Then we'll make a pass down by the river so they can drink before we go looking for the evening stop."

"That's what I wanted to ask you about," Willie said. "Do you want us to build a fire an' cook something or do we keep on going?"

"Plenty of time to cook and eat," Longarm said. "There's no hurry now."

"Good." Willie grinned and rubbed his belly with such transparent anticipation that Longarm was reminded of the bottomless capacity for food that all youngsters seemed to have.

He hoped he'd laid in enough supplies to keep this bunch of teenage hands satisfied, or at least close enough to it that they wouldn't outright mutiny between here and Ogallala.

"Go ahead and get at it," Longarm told him, "but remember, one man in the saddle and moving slow around the herd at all times. Right?"

"You bet." Willie wheeled his horse and cantered back toward the others while Longarm, moving much more cautiously in front of their little herd, began to ease the leaders to a halt.

Chapter 10

Longarm puffed on his cheroot with satisfaction. A smoke always tasted good after a meal. Supper was over, Willie and Roy were out on the first nighthawk shift, and Harvey was hunkered down by the fire waiting for the night's pot of coffee to boil. The coffee would be stout enough to stimulate a whore's cold heart by the time Longarm and Harvey were wakened for the late watch, but it would be almighty welcome then. Longarm's thoughts were on the bottle of Maryland rye in his saddlebags. One pull on it and then to sleep. Not a whole lot of sleeping got done when a small crew was trailing even the smallest herd. Holcroft's crowd a mile or so ahead should be nearly as weary after two days on the trail.

"Somebody coming, Tom," Harvey said. The kid had good ears. Longarm had thought his own hearing was good—there were times when it damn well had to be—but he had to cock his head and concentrate on listening before he could hear the approach of the horses Harvey had already detected.

Longarm stood and threw the stub of his cheroot into the coals left from the evening fire. "Damn it," he muttered, loud enough so that Harvey could hear and get the point, "that's the both of them coming in. They ought to know better than for both of them to leave the herd at once."

Harvey listened closely for a moment more and shook his head. "Can't be them," he said. "Three horses, at the least. Maybe four."

"Are you sure?"

Harvey shrugged. "Maybe not, but it sounds to me like the same beat as I used to hear back home whenever old Mr. Baldwin would come showing off with his coach an' four. Sure does sound like it."

Longarm listened again. As the hoofbeats came closer he was able to distinguish the sounds better. Three horses. So it wasn't Willie and Roy, unless they'd found a stray horse somewhere and wanted to keep it for a pet. Longarm stood and waited for the riders to reach the camp.

The riders stopped well outside the circle of light given off by the low fire. Two stayed where they were while one rode in without calling out or waiting for a welcome.

Longarm had seen the man before. He was one of the hands—bodyguards was more like it—who had been with Joe Holcroft the evening Longarm spoke with the boss driver. The man's expression did nothing to make Longarm believe that they had come to pay a neighborly call.

Convention and common courtesy required that Longarm, as the boss in this camp, should invite the guest to dismount and have a cup of coffee. Instead Longarm kept his jaw set. He folded his arms and nodded a greeting of sorts to the tall, lean Holcroft rider.

The man dismounted anyway and left his horse ground-reined. He walked to the fire and stood over it, facing Longarm across it. Harvey took a look at the stranger and apparently decided that the coffee could do its boiling without his help. He backed off and went off into the shadows to his bedroll without a word.

The man looked down at the coffee pot Harvey had been tending. The water was just beginning to boil. He hunkered down next to it and glanced toward the tin cup Harvey had left nearby.

"If I decide to offer you some," Longarm said, "I'll let you know."

The man's eyes came up to lock on Longarm's with a cold, unconcealed intensity that would have intimidated all but the most competent of men, or the most foolish. Longarm yawned and scratched his belly. That put his hand conveniently close to the grips of his Colt. The stranger grunted softly to himself and stood.

"Was there something you wanted?" Longarm asked.

"Something Mr. Holcroft wants," the man said. "He wants to know why you've been dogging us the last couple days."

"If he wants to ask me something he can come and ask it," Longarm said. "I don't owe explanations to hey-boys like you."

There was something about this lean man, something in the arrogant way he carried himself, that grated on Longarm. The plain and simple fact was that Longarm didn't like the son of a bitch.

Holcroft's gunny stiffened at the accusation that he was a hey-boy. His eyes narrowed and tension pulled at his shoulders.

Longarm was not even thinking about him, though. One overconfident gunslick was not going to worry him. He was thinking about the two men still sitting out there in the darkness. Longarm had no doubt at all that he could handle this one. The question was what would come afterward. There was a tightening in his own shoulders, and already he was planning which direction to move and roll. Afterward.

"Marty!" a voice called from the night.

The tall man facing Longarm flinched, and Longarm nearly pulled iron in reaction to the slight movement.

"What?" the tall man answered angrily. His eyes did not leave Longarm.

"Back off."

There was the sound of another horse approaching, and a second rider came into view.

Longarm waited until that man was easily visible before he glanced toward the rider. And even then his peripheral vision was still concentrated on the man named Marty, just in case.

"Back off, Marty. You, too, Tom."

Both Longarm and Marty relaxed a little. Longarm remained wary but no longer quite on the hair-trigger edge.

"It's me, Tom. Goose. You remember?"

"Hell, yes, I remember you, Goose." Longarm grinned. "Still owe you a drink, as I recall."

Goose Coe was the man who had been with Longarm when that idiot named Dave tried to attack them both with an axe. The same fellow who hadn't even considered saying anything to the police once Dave was dead. Yes, Longarm remembered him, and found it interesting if unexpected that Goose was with Holcroft's crew.

"Come down off that nag, Goose, and pour yourself a cup." He said nothing about including Marty in the invitation. Then he gave in and added, "You, too, and whoever's still out there."

Marty seemed to think about that for a moment. Then he shrugged. He bent and helped himself to the cup on the ground and poured some of the weak, steaming coffee into it. Longarm found extra cups for Goose and the third man and himself. The visit was likely to empty this pot. Harvey would have to make another one for the overnight coffee.

"So what the hell are you doin' here, Tom?" Goose asked when they all had coffee and the third man had been introduced as Leon.

"Nothing mysterious," Longarm said. "I told your boss I need to get up to Ogallala. Tried to hook on with him myself, as your friend here knows. When that didn't work out, I got the thinking that maybe I could pick up a few dollars by doing the same thing as Holcroft but on a scale I could manage out of my pocket. You know. Pick up a few extra bucks. So I'm taking a few head of my own up there."

"Why are you hanging so close to us?" Marty asked.

"Two reasons," Longarm said. "One is that you boys've been up this trail before. So you'll know where the best grass and water can be found. The other is that I heard a rumor before I left Dodge. Heard there might be some Indian trouble on the way. They say a bunch of Cheyenne left the reservation down in the Nations and could be headed north. If I run into a bunch of them I'd rather do it when your guns are close too. Four men wouldn't stand up all that good against a couple hundred Cheyenne."

Marty snorted his contempt for anyone nervous enough to be bothered about a few hundred Indians. Longarm had no doubt at all that Marty had proven himself more than a few times in stand-up fights against other whites, but he doubted now that Marty had ever seen a pissed-off Cheyenne warrior. That was nothing to sneer at, and it was a damn good thing that there were no outbreak rumors around right now.

Goose accepted the story without question. He nodded and said to Marty, "Tom, here, he's all right. Me and him got acquainted back in Dodge." Goose grinned at his companion, who apparently was not also a friend. "I seen what Tom can do, Marty. You ain't. So I figure you ought to back off from him."

Marty glowered, first at Goose and then at Longarm. Goose's response was a chuckle. He was no more afraid of Marty than Longarm was. Longarm ignored the dark look and took out cheroots for himself and for Goose.

Leon seemed not to be paying attention to any of it.

And come to think of it, Longarm wondered, where the hell was Harvey? Probably stretched out in his bedroll with a blanket pulled up over his head. Longarm couldn't blame the kid. This was no game for children.

"If Mr. Holcroft has any problem with me following his herd, Goose, let me know about it. I'll back off a few more miles. But I'd still like to stay close enough that a raiding party would think twice about jumping either herd."

"I don't think he'll mind once I explain the facts to him," Goose said.

"I appreciate that, Goose." Longarm smiled. "Come the time that we hit Ogallala I'll have to find you and buy you that drink I promised. I haven't forgot."

After the visitors had left, while Longarm was putting together a fresh pot of coffee, he got to thinking about just what Goose had said.

Explain what facts to Holcroft?

That lame excuse about grass and water? Or the nonsense about an Indian rumor?

Neither of those was really all that convincing. And Goose's opinion seemed to be on a personal basis anyway. Tom Custis was all right, it seemed, because he and Goose had been together when Dave died. And their acquaintance had begun because Longarm—Tom Custis—did not want to be spotted by a local deputy back in Dodge that morning.

That was interesting, Longarm thought. Particularly from the gun-quick manner that Joe Holcroft's crew showed. Marty, Goose, even Leon to a lesser extent.

Cowhands could be a rowdy bunch, but they generally weren't all that much with a gun. Firearms, in fact, were positively frowned on around always-nervous cattle, and a bit of harmless target practice could get a hand fired off most ranches. Yet Holcroft's crowd seemed damned well able with their weapons.

Why? Unless Holcroft was not the honest drover everyone thought.

Longarm sighed and set the refilled coffee pot over the coals.

That, after all, was what he had come here to learn.

Longarm switched his saddle from the day horse to Tom Bradley's good gelding and paused to take a quick look around.

Everything seemed set and comfortable for the night. The herd was in good shape, strung out on the grass just about a thick stand of crackwillow. The Arkansas was a shallow expanse of rippled silver in the late afternoon sunlight, sandbars and an occasional snag showing above the surface frequently. They would be turning north away from it in another day or two if Longarm had been figuring the distances correctly.

Roy was out keeping an eye on the herd, hanging back away from them so as to not disturb them, just the way Longarm had taught him, while Willie and Harvey put together the evening meal.

While Longarm watched out of the corner of his eye Willie reached into the grub sack for the butt end of a slab of bacon and managed to keep Harvey from seeing while he pried a rock out of the baked soil and moved it just behind Harvey's heel. When Harvey rocked backward his boot heel caught on the stone and turned, dumping him onto his butt with a yelp, and a friendly scuffle was on. The youngsters spent so much energy in harmless horseplay that it was a damn good thing they had so much of it to spare. Eventually, he knew, they would get tired of wrestling and go back to cooking, and no harm done.

A magpie glided overhead with a loud, rasping squawk of protest that there were no scraps available. Tomorrow the gaudy black and white bird might find easier pickings in the abandoned camp, but not necessarily. Those boys could damn sure clean up on the edibles. That was why Longarm expected to get almighty little sleep tonight.

He had bought and packed what he honestly believed

should be food enough to last them to Ogallala, but already they were out of tinned beef and they were running damned low on bacon too. He was going to have to buy some more.

"I'm going to ride into town," Longarm told the boys, who had finished their wrestling match and were sitting on the ground now, dusty and tired and looking happy.

"Town?" Willie asked. He sounded hopeful of an invitation to go along. "I didn't know there was a town near."

"About two miles upriver," Longarm said. "You could see the smoke from chimneys when we topped that last little rise on the way down to the riverbank."

"I didn't notice," Willie admitted.

"It's the sort of thing you learn to watch for. I won't be back for supper," Longarm told them, "and don't bother to save anything for me. I'll eat something there and be back in time for nighthawk."

"If you aren't," Harvey said, "I can handle it alone. I know what to do now."

"You do, but I'll be back."

"Yes, sir." Harvey looked a little disappointed, like he would rather show off his growing confidence and tend to things by himself tonight. Longarm had to admit that the boys were shaping into a pretty good crew after less than a week on the road.

"Don't forget . . ." Longarm started to say as he stepped into the saddle. Then he chopped the words off. He had been about to remind them to relieve Roy on herd watch so Roy could eat too. But that wasn't necessary. They wouldn't forget.

"What?"

"Nothing." He clamped a cheroot between his teeth, lighted it, then took up the reins and nudged the horse into motion toward the Holcroft herd that lay between their camp and whatever town it was that lay ahead. "I'll see you later."

"Okay, Tom." It had taken him a few days to break them

102

of the habit of calling him Mr. Custis, but now they seemed proud of being able to call the boss by his first name. Good kids, Longarm thought. He had been lucky with them.

He rode between the shallow flow of the Arkansas with its deceptively lazy flow—a mild-mannered surface that frequently hid a bottom unstable with quicksand and potholes—and the hugely sprawling Holcroft herd. One of the Holcroft riders waved to him and Longarm returned the greeting. It was growing too dark for Longarm to see if it might have been Goose Coe.

The town lay another mile ahead on the opposite bank of the Arkansas. There was no bridge, of course, but a firm-bottomed ford had been markekd out with stakes driven into the riverbed. Longarm splashed the horse across the ford and entered the double row of buildings that made up the small community. The wide area between them apparently was the town's main and only street.

A man leaning against the front of a harness-maker's shop eyed Longarm with interest but no hostility. Longarm reined the horse toward him and stopped.

"Could you point me to a mercantile where I might buy some supplies?"

"Fourth place on your right."

Longarm thanked him and started to turn away.

"But Jim's closed now," the man added.

"Damn," Longarm muttered. "I really need to get some things."

"You might find him, though, an' I daresay Jim'd open for you if you got cash money to pay with."

"Where do you think I could find him?"

"The saloon, most likely. He takes his supper there most nights since his missus died. Ask for Jim Berwick." The man smiled and shifted a chew from one side of his jaw to the other. "Or look for a cueball. Only hair Jim's got is his eyebrows and whatever sticks outa his nose."

"Thanks," Longarm said again.

"On your left. Next to last place in town."

"I appreciate it."

Longarm rode on. He would have been able to spot the saloon easily enough without directions. The hitch rails in front of it and on both sides of the place were crowded. Longarm added his mount to the lineup and went inside.

The place was of good size, and it needed to be. Apparently a good many locals made it their nightly stop. In addition to the local people, Longarm could recognize several faces at the far end of the bar as coming from Holcroft's crew. The Holcroft men were in a group of half a dozen, and he assumed that all of them were from the tail drive.

The locals were about evenly divided between the bar and a number of tables scattered across the floor. A penny-ante card game was in progress at one of the tables, but meals had been laid out at the others. Longarm guessed that the saloon was as close as the town came to having a regular restaurant.

There was no sign of a bald man who might be Berwick, so Longarm found an empty table and sat. The bowls of stew that were being served smelled good to him after the rough fare he and the boys had been able to cook for themselves.

"You can set there as long as you like," a man at the next table told him, "but if you wanta eat you got to go to the door yonder and ask. I'll mind your chair for you while you're gone."

"Thank you kindly." Nice folks in this town, Longarm thought. He dropped his hat onto the table to show that it was occupied and went to the door that had been indicated. He tapped on it lightly. When that produced no response he knocked again, louder this time.

"Coming," a voice called from the other side.

The door swung open. A woman stood there with a steaming bowl of stew already in her hands. "Here you . . ." Recognition widened her eyes and put a broad, happy smile onto her face. "Lo—"

"Custis," Longarm said quickly and rather too loudly. "It's me all right, Jenny. Long Tom Custis. I'm surprised you'd remember."

The woman blinked in confusion for a moment, then seemed to catch on. "Not remember you? Go on now, Long Tom Custis." So she had gotten the message. She wasn't going to tip anyone. At least not right now. At least not by accident.

"Could we . . . talk, Jenny? As soon as possible?"

She hesitated for only a moment. "Sure." She hesitated again. "Tom."

"Thanks." Automatically he accepted the bowl of stew she pushed into his hands. Jenny backed into the kitchen and allowed the door to swing shut in Longarm's face.

He turned and carried his supper back to the cable. The Holcroft men turned their heads to watch his progress through the saloon.

But that was only natural, wasn't it? Surely they couldn't have noticed anything about that brief exchange with Jenny.

Surely not.

Chapter 11

The stew had smelled good. It probably tasted good as well. Longarm was too preoccupied to notice. He ate mechanically, keeping an eye on the kitchen door. From time to time someone would knock there to request a meal. Invariably the knock was answered by Jenny Nichol.

Jenny Nichol. He remembered her well. How she had come here he had no idea, but she used to live in the Indian Territories, where her father ran a store under license from the Choctaw Nation.

Longarm had met her in the line of duty when a group of unusually enterprising criminals tried to organize a monopoly on the sale of illegal whiskey to Indians. They had tried, without any long-term success, to force Cy Nichol to sell their product. Nichol had helped Longarm put the crowd behind bars. At the time, Longarm had been a young and fairly inexperienced deputy. Jenny had been a *very* young and inexperienced—but damned pretty—girl

107

in whose home he had been staying.

She was still damned pretty, he thought, now that the shock of recognition had passed, but not so young. Probably not so inexperienced either. As Longarm recalled, he had contributed more to her experience than decency should have permitted.

Now, in this no-name little town off in a distant corner of Kansas, Jenny Nichol was in a position to expose him to Joe Holcroft's men if she was not cautious. Or if she wanted to. As he recalled, there had been a great deal of weeping and recrimination when the young deputy had ridden off to his next assignment instead of settling down in her daddy's business.

He hoped there were no lingering hard feelings about that long-ago separation.

The supper crowd slacked off and the drinkers got down to some serious elbow-bending. The Holcroft men, keeping to themselves at one end of the bar, were already doing some heavy drinking. Longarm finished his stew and went to the bar. The place did not offer anything as elegant as Maryland rye, so he contented himself with beer and a pickled egg to pass the time. Eventually, when it had been quite a while since the last knock on the kitchen door, Jenny opened the door a few inches and motioned for Longarm to go outside and come around to the back of the building. She popped back out of sight before he had time to respond or to read her expression. He settled his bill and did as Jenny wanted.

There was a back door to the saloon building. She was waiting outside it with a shawl wrapped around her shoulders. He thought she seemed nervous.

He felt a bit shy himself after all these years. He didn't know whether to shake her hand or give her a kiss. He settled for a smile and the preoccupation of lighting a cheroot.

"How have you been, Longarm?" she asked in a soft whisper. Lamplight coming through a window off the kitchen fell across her face, and she seemed as young and lovely as Longarm remembered her to have been.

"Tom. Please."

"Sorry."

"I've been fine, thank you. And you?"

She shrugged. "Have you missed me? Tom?"

"Yes."

Jenny laughed. The nervousness was gone now. She might even have been enjoying herself. "That's a lie, if a sweet one. You won't have thought of me in years. Nor I of you, if that is what's worrying you. But it *is* nice to see you again." She took his hand in hers and pulled him away from the back step, leading him away from the row of buildings and past a scattered jumble of houses that surrounded the town until the lights of the village were dim, and they were surrounded only by prairie grasses and starlight.

She talked while they slowly walked. She had married. Her husband had been a cowboy, honest and earnest and hard-working. They had saved up a little money and four years ago came out here to take up land and start their own small ranch. It was working out until his horse took a fall and her cowboy got himself gored by a balky milk cow that resented having her calf taken away from her. Not even by a range bull, but by a damn milk cow. The puncture had festered, and her cowboy died after forty-eight days of agony.

They'd had a child, but she died, too, of cholera. Jenny shrugged as if it had been long enough ago that the pain had gone, but there was something in her eyes that denied that.

Now she worked for Fred, cooking and serving meals to his customers. The business with the knocking on the door was so she would not have to step into the saloon, which would not have been decent, even in a town where there was no proper cafe for people to go to when they were hungry.

109

It would have been better if she could open her own place, but she had no money to build with and Fred seemed to want her there where he could keep an eye on her. Fred was in love with her.

Longarm had seen the bartender, guessed that the man was Fred, and understood why Jenny would not be enthused about marrying him.

"What about you, Long Tom Custis?"

"Same old deal."

"You're working now?"

"Yes."

"I'm glad," she said.

"Really?"

"Of course, dear. It proves that no one else has been able to capture you either. It would be nice, about now, if you could lie and tell me that no one else has meant more to you . . . than I did. Once."

Longarm did not have time to answer. She turned to him. His arms went around her, and his lips found hers.

She trembled slightly and pressed herself hard against him. He remembered now that she had been inexperienced then, but every bit as eager as he. She was every bit as eager now.

Her mouth opened, and her tongue explored him.

Almost of its own volition his hand found and cupped her breast, and Jenny moaned.

She began to fumble at the buttons of his trousers.

There was no one near. No one to see. The lights of the town seemed distant. They were as alone on the prairie as if they had been miles from civilization. The night air was soft and cool on his flesh.

Longarm lowered her gently to the ground, and Jenny seemed to melt to his touch.

Something was holding up the progress of the Holcroft herd up ahead. The long, strung-out line of cattle was pushing together into a near-solid mass.

110

They were slowing down too. Longarm's little herd had not increased their pace at all, but they were much closer now to the Holcroft drag. The last of the Holcroft riders, with their remuda and chuck wagon, were less than a quarter of a mile away.

More interesting, Longarm could see some of the flank men signalling with their hats. All but a necessary few of the Holcroft riders were leaving their positions and riding forward.

Longarm turned and motioned for Willie to come up from the east flank and join him. They had turned north away from the river yesterday and were now lining out for Nebraska, more or less following the state line that separated Kansas from Colorado. Willie bumped his horse into a lope and came forward.

"Yeah, Tom?"

"There's something wrong up ahead, and I don't want our herd mixing into theirs. You men—" Longarm was careful never to bruise their pride by calling them boys—"bunch our cattle and hold them here until I see what's up."

The boy looked toward the sky, to where the sun was still climbing. "Do you want us to go ahead an' build a noon fire and let them graze?"

"I don't know yet. If I'm not back in half an hour, say, go ahead and start the cooking. Meantime you can let the beeves graze, but don't let them drift into the Holcroft herd. Okay?"

"You can count on us, Tom."

"I know I can." He started forward, then paused. "Pork chops and dried-apple pie for dinner?"

Willie laughed. Longarm never had found that store-keeper back along the river, and now they were down to eating beans for a main course with a spoonful of beans for a vegetable and perhaps a dab of beans for dessert.

Longarm put his horse into a canter and swung wide around the Holcroft cattle so he would not disturb them.

The few hands who were remaining with the herd ignored him as he passed. Their attention was forward along the jostling, grumpy herd. Longarm was reminded again that this was just too big a herd to move comfortably in a single mass.

He topped one of the countless low, barely recognizable rises that rolled endlessly forward in this country. Now he could better see what the delay was.

Someone had gone and strung a wire fence smack across the public droving road.

The fencing must surely have been done within the past few weeks, the past month at the longest, because Holcroft and probably others as well had been up the road no longer ago than that.

Holcroft and most of his riders were gathered in a knot on one side of the fence. A small group of men with two heavy wagons and a few saddle horses faced them from the other side of the wire.

"I don't know anything about your so-called rights, mister," Holcroft was saying as Longarm came up to them, "but I know that this is a public road. Set down by the Congress of these United States *as* a road. You can file all the shitty little squatters' claims you want. The fact remains, this particular piece of ground is free for any man to travel on, cattle and all. And that is what I intend to do here."

"Set one fookin' foot on my land, laddie, an' it's the last fookin' step ye take." The man who spoke had a Scots burr on his tongue and a Sharps carbine in his hands. He looked angry. "I jus' got this fence builded, an' I'll na have you tearin' it doon."

"If you don't want it torn down," Holcroft said patiently, "don't build the son of a bitch on public ground."

"'Tis mine land, laddie, not yorn. I staked it an' I claimed it an' I'll stand on it to the death," the Scot insisted.

"I don't want it to come to that," Holcroft said. "But I don't have time to argue with you about it. Just lay the wires down. I'll drive my cattle over your damn fence and on to Ogallala. You can take it up with whoever your local law is. That's up to you and them. I don't want to mix into it. I just want to get this herd to Ogallala."

Longarm thought Holcroft sounded remarkably—and, in truth, unexpectedly—reasonable about the request. Especially in view of the hard gunslicks who rode for him. Holcroft's crew was capable of wiping out the Scot and every last man with him and probably never having to break a sweat to get the job done.

There were only the Scot and four other men on the far side of the fence and none of them looked any better than a low average for hard-knocks experience.

Holcroft had eight men backing him up now, and there were four more back with the herd who would surely come fogging it to help if they heard gunfire.

Besides, as Longarm damn well knew, the Scot and his people were in the wrong here.

Joe Holcroft had spoken the simple truth when he told the stubborn Scot that this road had been exempted from Homestead Act filings by order of Congress. There had been so much trouble between Texas drovers and Kansas farmers back East that Congress had acted on the Ogallala Trail to specifically avoid such problems here.

And now here this idiot Scot was, making a fool of himself and a mockery of that law.

"All I want to do," Holcroft said calmly, "is pass through. Whether the land is yours or public land I won't argue. You can take that up elsewhere. I just want to *cross* it."

"Go around," the Scot snapped.

"I haven't time to go around," Holcroft said. He still sounded patient, but there was an edge to his voice now. "Besides, you've fenced off the water hole my cattle need

113

today. The water is every bit as much mine as it is yours, and I need it."

"Ha!" the Scot snapped with a grin, as if some point had just been proven in his favor. "It's na just my fence ye want t' roon. It's my graze an' my water too ye'd steal. Go around, I say."

Holcroft shook his head. He turned and gave Marty a sad, weary look of exasperation. Then he turned back to face the Scot. "I've tried to reason with you, mister. You won't have that. If you won't let me lay your wire down, I'll just have to cut it." Holcroft motioned with his right hand, and Marty nodded.

The lean foreman dismounted and moved toward the wire. "Bring me those nippers, Leon."

"Ye'll not!" the Scott roared. He stood in the wagon he had been driving—a wagon that was nearly empty except for a few spools of wire and some kegs that probably had held staples—and shook his Sharps menacingly toward Marty.

Marty ignored him. He stopped at the fence and examined the wire attached to cedar posts that had been set into the hard, sun-baked soil with a monumental expenditure of sweat.

Leon reached into his saddlebags and produced a short-handled set of wire cutters. He kneed his horse forward to hand the cutters down to Marty.

"No!" the Scot bellowed.

He clawed for the hammer of the Sharps, and even from where Longarm sat he could hear the distinct clack of oiled metal as the hammer dog engaged the sear.

Behind the Scot his own men watched uncertainly, obviously not sure if they should reach for the few revolvers and carbines they had or if they should let their boss handle it.

Holcroft's men had no such hesitation.

Marty's hand swept a single-action Colt from his holster, and behind him every rider of the crew was reaching too.

The Scot moved as if to bring the Sharps to his shoulder, and Marty fired.

Behind him half a dozen other guns roared, sending a sound like thunder across the grass.

The bullets ripped into the Scot, riddling him from throat to belt buckle. The man was driven backward by the impact of the slugs. He staggered, trying to keep his feet, and a look of astonishment flickered briefly across his whiskered face.

Then the light of life went out of his glazing eyes and he toppled forward, off the wagon seat and onto the ground.

His men were as immobile as if they had been frozen in place.

"No," Marty barked, and Longarm realized that one of the Holcroft men had been about to shoot one of the dead Scot's people. The Holcroft man jerked the muzzle of his colt toward the sky but remained ready, his revolver cocked and his eyes on the group facing them across the fence.

One of the Scot's men looked like he was going to be sick. The others were being very careful to make no moves that could in any way be considered threatening.

"Cut the wire, Marty," Holcroft said in a calm, steadying voice.

"Yes, sir." Again Leon moved his horse forward. Marty took the cutters from him and began to nip the wire, strand by strand. The sound of the steel cutting blades snipping closed seemed very loud.

"Gather your dead," Holcroft said. "We won't bother you."

"Yes . . . yes, sir," one of the suddenly unemployed fence builders said.

Holcroft looked toward his own men as if to caution them and for the first time he noticed Longarm there.

"You have any problem with this, Mr. Custis?"

115

"It was self-defense," Longarm said.

"You'll testify to that if there's an inquiry?"

Longarm rubbed his chin and thought for a moment. "I would. But if the law comes around . . ." He shrugged his shoulders and gave Holcroft a look of apology. "I think I'm busy that day."

Holcroft stared at him for a moment, then nodded. "Fair enough, Mr. Custis."

When Longarm got back to his own herd he was a little bit disappointed. The cattle were strung out in much too loose a group for being so close to the big Holcroft herd. The boys had not done a good job of keeping them together.

Obviously the boys realized their error as soon as the boss was back in sight to watch them, because now they were busy circling the herd and pushing the animals into a tight gather.

Chapter 12

It had been a fair fight, Longarm reflected late that night. The Scotsman had been in the wrong, but he pushed the issue anyway. And Marty and his men finished it for him. If Longarm had to testify at an inquiry he would have to tell it exactly that way.

But the sheer waste of it rankled him. If things had been different—if he'd been able to drag out his badge and wave it under the Scot's nose before the shooting began—then that stubborn, belligerent, totally in the wrong Scotsman need not have died.

And that was what it finally came down to.

Deputy U. S. Marshal Custis Long could have stopped the whole affair with a few spoken words.

Sometime cattle drover Long Tom Custis, with his nervousness about the law and with a past he never mentioned, had just sat there watching, honestly not realizing that the damnfool Scot was going to push the issue against all right and against all reason—and, more important, against all common sense when he was outnumbered and outgunned and miles out of his own league even if the figures had been reversed. No, that fool had gone and pushed things far beyond the point that Deputy U. S. Marshal Custis Long would have thought possible.

So Longarm's cover story was intact but the Scot was dead and by now maybe even buried.

Longarm was feeling responsible for the fool's death. Because no matter how he reationalized it or tried to explain it to himself with the damned facts, the simple truth was that the Scotsman would still be alive right now if Longarm had spoken up and identified himself.

No matter who was right or who was wrong or how far and how fast things had gone beyond the point of reason, that was the truth of it. The man was dead. He would still be alive if only Longarm had identified himself as a federal officer.

Longarm cursed himself out loud, and a steer nearby, up for the middle-of-the-night stretch, snorted and wheeled aside, causing a momentary flurry of near-panic in the herd. Longarm cursed himself again, but more quietly this time, and remembered to resume the soft, monotonous crooning as he rode the wide circle around the sleeping herd. For a while there, preoccupied with his thinking and his regrets, he had quit the singing and so had nearly precipitated a stampede in the herd.

If one of the boys had done that Longarm would have chewed the kid's ass. Longarm made up for it by mentally chewing his own ass while he rode in a counterclockwise circle around the herd. But this time he remembered to sing to the cattle as he went.

Singing to a bunch of ignorant cattle!

The boys probably felt foolish as all billy-hell doing it. Longarm certainly had, back on that long-ago drive when he had been young and green and just learning the cow business. Back before he knew what it was to carry a badge and go out in the deliberate pursuit of other men.

At first he had even thought the older hands were pulling a joke on him when they told him he had to sing to the cows all night long. He thought it for sure but he did it anyway, because he had been ordered to.

Turned out there was a good reason for it.

Cattle, particularly cattle on the trail, far from their familiar home ground, were spooky sons of bitches. They were liable to take fright at anything or at nothing, and once they did they might sull up and refuse to budge or they might just as easily break into a panicked run for the horizon and not slow down for a day and a half.

The night herder's singing did two things to avoid that. For one, it let the cows know where he was, let them know that a man and horse were approaching so they wouldn't be startled or surprised and take off at the unexpected click of a horse's hoof on stone. The other reason was that the sounds of a lullaby genuinely seemed to soothe and calm them.

Weird, Longarm thought, but true. The damned critters actually seemed to like being sung to.

So night after night, the whole night through, no matter the trail or the danger of discovery by unfriendly humans, all through the cow country grown men rode around their herds singing to their cattle.

Anybody who didn't know the score on that would likely think it funny as hell. And of course they'd be right. It *was* funny as hell, but effective.

It was too dark a night for Longarm to see much. Not that he had to see all that much. He could trust the horse to make the circles for him.

Up ahead he could her Roy Garrett approaching, making the same slow circuits that Longarm was except in the opposite, clockwise direction so that they met and passed twice each time around the herd.

Roy seemed to have an ear for music that was every bit as poor as Longarm's and maybe even worse. He seemed not to have a handle on any of the modern tunes that a fellow might hear in the trail-town honkytonks and lacked either the imagination or the nerve to make up his own songs like so many of the trailhands did. So Roy always sang cradle tunes to the cattle, the sort of thing he would have heard from his mama when he was still in diapers. Longarm's preference ran to the sentimental marching songs of the recent conflict. At the moment Roy was mumbling an off-key version of "London Bridge"—a little livelier than most bovines preferred, although this crowd seemed to take to it well enough—while Longarm was extolling the virtues of Aura Lee. Both Willie and Harvey had a penchant for hymns, and voices that weren't too bad either.

Roy slowed his horse as he neared Longarm. Both stopped, knee to knee but facing in opposite directions.

"Smoke?" Longarm asked. As long as the cattle knew the riders were there, the strike of a match would not bother them.

"No thanks, but if you don't mind I'll pull it in for a cup o' that coffee."

"Go ahead." The rule was that no one left the herd without first informing the other of the need for it, so there would not be any confusion about something having gone wrong when the other rider failed to show up on the circuit. "But I hope you got a sharp knife on you. This time of morning the pot oughta be stout enough that you'll have to pry the stuff out in chunks."

"Need anything from the camp?"

"No, but don't be too long. I got to take a leak before too long."

"What do you think? Another hour?"

"Before I can take a leak? It better not be."

"Dang it, Tom, that isn't what I meant." Roy still seemed a bit uncertain about when the boss was joking with him and when Longarm was being serious.

"Yeah, about an hour," Longarm told him. It was the

120

junior nighthawk's job every morning to start the breakfast fire before the early-shift boys were shaken out of their bedrolls.

"I won't be long, Tom."

"Okay." Longarm lighted his cheroot and clucked to his horse, moving it back into the slow, walking pattern of the circle around the herd. He began singing again, this time a complicated, only partially remembered thing about some distant cowboy's favorite horse, Old Paint. The parts Longarm didn't remember did not matter anyway. He made up nonsense words to fill in the gaps and rode on through the chill pre-dawn, thinking as he went that he had abandoned a simpler life when he took to carrying a badge.

That wasn't to say that it was a better life, but it damn sure was a different one.

Still, as long as he *did* choose to carry that badge—and the responsibilities that went with it—he was just going to have to live with all the complications that came with the job, including the guilt. Like, for instance, the thought of a Scotsman who'd wanted to build a ranch of his own and instead put a permanent claim on six feet of west Kansas soil.

"It's shitty, Old Paint," Longarm sang softly, "but we'll do what we can."

Longarm rode into the town with the pack mule behind. This town at least had enough civic pride to put a sign up proclaiming its name, Rault City. They were getting so low on supplies thanks to the boys' eating habits that he had to resupply soon or start frying buffalo grass for breakfast.

Rault City was no bigger than the place down on the Arkansas where Jenny lived. Come to think of it, he never had found out what Jenny's last name was nowadays. This town had several saloons to choose from when he was ready for a drink, and it had a general mercantile that was still open for business in the early evening.

He'd learned his lesson about grabbing the local store-

121

keeper while he could, so he went first to the general store and bought enough bacon and tinned beef and flour and beans to last twice as many people for twice as long as he thought necessary. He realized that would probably be just about enough to get them to Ogallala.

There was no point in making the mule stand tied with a heavy pack on its back while he found himself a drink and a real meal, so he left the mule, horse, and sacks of supplies in the Rault City livery's corral, pumped the trough full of water, and paid a skinny youngster with a two-fisted Adam's apple two bits for an armload of prairie hay. "I won't be long," he told the kid.

"Take your time, mister. No extra charge unless you want 'em groomed or put under cover."

"No need for that."

Rault City boasted a real cafe in addition to the extra saloon over the town to the south, and Longarm treated himself to a good meal with not a boiled bean on the table, and managed to do it without once feeling guilty about what the boys were having to eat back at the camp.

When he finished and came back out onto the street, the evening trade had arrived. Both saloons were filling up, and in front of the nearer place were tied seven horses that he recognized from the Holcroft remuda. So they had a shift in town, too, either to resupply or just to have some drinks while the liquor was available.

Longarm headed in that direction. He crossed the street, having to wait once while a pair of locals trotted by and again to let a light wagon past.

He had to admit to paying a little more attention to the wagon than he had to the horseback cowboys. The wagon was being driven by a rather attractive red-headed girl who was handling her team with more determination than skill.

Pert, he thought, with a figure that no amount of ruffles and pleats could hide. She pulled the wagon to a stop behind the Holcroft crew's horses and showed more than a hint of ankle as she climbed down off the rig. The ankle was slim and shapely. Longarm was not fond of thick ankles that looked like chunks of stovewood stuck into a shoe.

The redhead left her wagon in the middle of the street there with her team untethered and grabbed her handbag off the seat. Longarm had to detour around the tailgate of the wagon in order to reach the door of the saloon. The redhead sure seemed in a hurry about something.

He reached the front door of the saloon and pushed it open.

The redhead pushed her way past him and went inside. She damn sure didn't look like the kind who would be going into a place like that. She looked downright respectable. Not that it was any of his business, anyway.

She stopped in front of him, just inside the doorway, blocking his path so he had to stop too. He reached for a cheroot.

"You! There at the bar. Yes, you, damn you."

Amusement pulled at the corners of Longarm's eyes. It looked like this girl had the temper to go with her hair. He guessed he was fixing to listen to her bless out her husband or boyfriend or whatever for being in a den of iniquity when the poor fellow ought to be home tending to business. Longarm thumbed a match aflame and applied it to the tip of his cheroot, pretending to pay no attention to the young lady who was blocking his way, but eavesdropping anyway.

"Killers. You're a bunch of damn killers," the redhead accused.

The men at the bar, including the Holcroft riders, seemed as confused by the accusation as Longarm was. They stood where they were and stared at her.

The girl fumbled with the drawstrings of her handbag, snatched the thing open, and reached inside. When her hand emerged again she was holding a little nickel-plated break-action revolver, a Smith probably. It was just a little bit of a thing, likely no bigger than a .32 rimfire. But that was damn sure big enough to kill a man just as dead as a more manly .44-40.

She held the thing in both hands, muzzle extended toward the Holcroft men, jaw set with grim determination, eyes squinting nearly closed.

She had gone suddenly quite pale. Longarm was aware of the pattern of freckles that draped over the bridge of her nose.

He could see how white her knuckles were where they gripped the gun, and could see as well the tightening of her finger as she hauled back on the spur trigger.

The hammer of the little gun was cocked. Another bit of pressure . . .

Longarm reached forward and put his thumb between the hammer and frame of the little gun.

The girl's finger tripped the sear, but the hammer fell harmlessly on Longarm's thumb, giving it a mildly painful pinch but not doing any worse damage than that.

He twisted gently and disengaged the little revolver from the girl's suddenly weak grip.

She gave him a brief look, aghast, although whether with him for stopping her or herself for what she had nearly done, he could not be sure. Then she whirled and raced out of the saloon. He could hear her break into loud sobs as she ran back to her wagon and scrambled awkwardly onto the seat. She grabbed up her lines and jumped the team into a run, charging off down the street and into the night.

Longarm was left in the doorway with a puzzled look on his face and the little Smith in his hand. He disengaged the thing from his thumb, let the hammer safely down, and with a shrug tossed it onto the nearest table.

"What the hell was that all about?" he asked.

"MacVay's widow," someone said.

That more or less explained things, he supposed, if MacVay was a recently dead Scotsman.

124

Longarm went to the bar and the Holcroft men moved over to join him.

"You'd be Tom Custis?" one of them asked him.

"That's right."

"Drink up, Tom. Your money's no good in here tonight. Whatever you want's on us."

Chapter 13

They drove on to the north, Longarm with his little herd and his crew of inexperienced youngsters hanging close behind the sprawling Holcroft herd. Eighteen, twenty miles a day.

The pace was slow for a man on horseback but remarkably fast for a trail herd, especially for a herd as large and ungainly to manage as Holcroft's bunch. Fifteen miles would have been a more likely average, but Holcroft did not settle for that, pushing his cattle early off their noon grazing even when there was excellent grass to be had and getting the most out of the available daylight hours.

The man seemed to be in a hurry, Longarm thought, although the reason eluded him. A slower pace of travel, with more time to graze and to drink, would have meant fatter and therefore higher priced cattle at the Ogallala end. Surely Holcroft was operating on too slim a profit margin to risk any reductions. Unless, of course, the man knew something about expected changes in the Chicago beef market prices and had some kind of deadline to meet.

That possibility existed. Otherwise, though, Longarm could think of no good reason for the continued speed.

Still, Longarm was having some doubts about Joe Holcroft and about Billy Vail's suspicions concerning the man.

Everything the man had done so far had been entirely legal, as far as Longarm could see. Not just under federal law either, but under any and all laws that Longarm knew of.

Billy Vail's interest was admittedly personal. The marshal's suspicions were based perhaps more on wishful thinking—or as easily on a sense of genuine concern—than on any real evidence or knowledge.

It was exactly that that hung Longarm out on the same limb where Billy was now dangling.

Even so, Longarm was beginning to have his doubts about his own early doubts.

Joe Holcroft was commencing to come across as exactly the drover he claimed to be. He'd paid off as promised time and time again this summer past. His men were a hard and quick crew, but back there at the illegal fence they had clearly been in the right. Still, they hadn't jumped the Scotsman. They had only defended themselves when it became necessary. Longarm could fault no man for that.

The plain and simple truth was—and it came hard for him to make the admission, even to himself—that Longarm was beginning now to have doubts about Billy Vail's objectivity in this assignment.

The whole thing was beginning to smack a shade too much of personal vendetta. And there was no place in the law for that.

Still, the job was not done. It would serve no purpose to turn aside now. Ogallala was just a matter of days up the road, and the herd of cattle Longarm had "borrowed" from the army had to be disposed of somewhere. Easier in Ogallala than back in now-distant Dodge.

So Longarm and his boys pressed on, eating the dust of the Holcroft herd and giving the youngsters something to tell their children about once the steel rails had reached the last far-flung domains of the range and the trail drive had become a thing of history.

At least now the going was sociable.

After that incident at Rault City, and probably with Goose Coe's urging too, the Holcroft crew had dropped their stand-off attitude toward Longarm and his boys.

Now whenever one bunch was in sight of the other there was sure to be a friendly wave or a shout of encouragement or, if there was time, a brief meeting to offer chews of tobacco or a joke.

When a steer consigned to the Holcroft herd took a tumble and broke a foreleg, Longarm and his boys received half a haunch of fresh meat that was more than welcome when sliced into thick slabs and fried crisp and brown in the steer's own tallow.

The miles and the dust and the grass rolled behind them past Stateline. Longarm might also have been recognized there and so avoided the place, but Goose apparently found time for a visit to the Stateline because soon afterward the gun-quick trailhand showed up at Longarm's campfire with a pint of bourbon in his pocket and a fistful of excellent cigars to share.

A pint shared among five men provided little whiskey for any one of the drinkers, just about enough to put a sense of warmth into a man's belly, but the drinks were enough to make Roy Garrett woozy and tongue-tied and to get Willie Jones and Harvey Moelken downright tiddly. Both of them were weaving in their saddles for the early watch, and Longarm damn sure hoped there would be no trouble with the herd this night.

Goose Coe gave Longarm a look of amused understanding and saluted Longarm with the nearly empty bottle. "T' those of us who've been there an' those who've yet to learn. Right, Tom?"

"Right," Longarm agreed solemnly.

Goose laughed, and the two older men split the last swallow in the jug.

Goose handed over another of the excellent cigars and lighted it for Longarm. Longarm drew deep of the smoke and took it out of his jaw to admire it. The plump corona was as good as ever Longarm had tasted, with an exceptionally pale wrapper leaf and the finest quality filler. Much better, in fact, than Longarm's own expensive cheroots.

"Ten cents each but worth every penny," Goose said with pleasure. He seemed genuinely glad to be able to share whatever good fortune had led to the purchase.

"None better," Longarm agreed. But instead of paying attention to the cigar now he was wondering how a trail-droving cowhand could come up with the funds to buy ten-cent cigars. For a man whose income was probably a dollar a day, ten-cent cigars could burn up his entire payday and leave nothing extra for drinks or a bit of womanizing.

Yet Goose seemed happy to be able to share with Longarm and his crew besides.

That was a small puzzlement, though, and likely not an important one. Longarm forgot about it for the moment and concentrated on enjoying the superior smoke while he had the chance. The late-night herd watch would be coming up soon enough, and then it would be back to monotony and off-key lullabies for the drowsy cattle.

"Thank you, Goose."

"Any time, Tom."

Longarm pulled his horse to a stop and stood in the stirrups. He cocked his head to one side and concentrated on listening.

There was a sound in the air like distant thunder, but there was hardly a cloud visible anywhere from horizon to horizon. Besides, the low, rumbling noise seemed to be

130

coming from just ahead, from the rise where the drag end of the Holcroft herd had just disappeared a few minutes before.

Longarm turned and looked back toward Harvey. The kid had about the best ears of anybody Longarm knew. He had heard it, too, even though he was back along the flank of the herd and would have been bothered some by the low, continuous noises made by their own cattle.

Harvey, too, was standing in his stirrups trying to concentrate. He gave Longarm a questioning look, then shook his head. He could hear it but he did not know what it was.

It was getting louder now. Closer? Not so much like thunder, really. Maybe closer to the sound of a runaway ore cart deep underground.

Runaway?

Longarm felt a chill cut through him despite the heat of the sun on his shoulders.

He recognized it now. It was something a man didn't want to hear many times in one life.

Longarm whirled his horse back toward his crew and snatched off his hat to wave at them. "Turn! Turn 'em!"

Too late.

The first wild-eyed, panic-stricken Holcroft beeves burst into sight on top of the near ridge and raced down toward his own little herd.

Behind those first few streamed five thousand more.

Stampede!

Five thousand fear-blinded cattle on a dead run. Heads high, eyes glassy, horns clattering, nostrils fluttering wide, hooves pulverizing anything and everything they passed over.

There was no sign of the Holcroft drag riders.

"Leave ours!" Longarm shouted, bellowing in an effort to overcome the rising thunder-swell of raw sound that preceded the stampeding herd. "We got to turn the run."

He had no idea if any of the boys had been able to hear. Anyway, it was too late to give instructions about what should be done with their own little herd. The borrowed annuity beeves were already reacting to the sight of the onrushing Holcroft herd. Longarm's cattle stopped to stamp their forefeet and raise their heads for a moment. Then the infectious panic hit them. They whirled, quick as cats where a moment before they had been docile and plodding, and jumped into a hard run toward the southeast.

There was nothing out there to stop them, Lord knew. Nothing but a hundred miles or more of rolling grass and maybe a puny wire fence or two until they would get to the Arkansas.

Not that they would ever get that far, damn it. They would die of sheer exhaustion before they reached that point. And they very likely would run until they died if no one stopped them.

Longarm turned his horse out of the path of the stampede, jabbing its flanks with the big-roweled Mexican spurs and lifting it into a belly-down race with the flying longhorns.

He continued to sit upright on the animal, guiding it with one hand and with the other fumbling behind him for the tie-strings that held his slicker behind the cantle.

The strings would not come loose. Fuck it. No time. He grabbed a handful of oilcloth and yanked, snapping the whangs and pulling the slicker free. He shook it out and used it as a flag to try to scare the damned cattle even more, trying to scare them away from his position on the right flank so as to turn them aside.

If they could get the leaders turned, get the whole strung-out herd running in a wide circle, it might then be possible to squeeze in on them from the outside until the herd milled and turned in on itself, until it was a solid mob of cattle too closely packed to run any more.

Longarm raced past an uncomprehending Willie Jones and flew by an equally confused Roy Garrett. He was leaning forward in the saddle now, putting all of his weight

132

over the horse's withers to give it the freest possible movement and the most possible speed.

"Hyah! Hyah! Hee-*yahh!*" There was no hope of getting the stupid cattle to pay attention. The shouting was for the horse's benefit, trying to get the last scrap of speed from it. He wished as he rode that he was on Tom Bradley's much better horse.

The leaders of the Holcroft herd had ripped past him almost before he had time to react and before his horse could gain the speed to head them. Now they were running probably fifty yards ahead of him, charging dead on toward the impossibly distant river.

"Hyah, horse, you son of a bitch." He waved the slicker, but only the nearest of the cattle flinched away from it to jostle deeper into the packed mass of terror-stricken animals. The leaders ran on unaffected.

"Hyah, horse." He spurred the animal again and again, but if it gained ground on the racing cattle it was too slowly for him to see any result.

His own little herd had virtually disappeared, swallowed up in the near-solid herd of crazed cattle.

"Hyah, you son of a bitch."

The damned horse just wasn't gaining. Worse, it stumbled once, righted itself at a full-out run, and raced on. But the momentary change in direction was nearly enough to unseat Longarm as he leaned precariously forward over the fool animal's neck.

If he went down now . . . Time enough to fret about that later. He laid the steel into the horse's flanks again but got no more speed, only an angry shake of the beast's head.

"What do I do, Tom?"

Harvey Moelken was riding right beside him. Riding as comfortable and easy as if they were out for a Sunday canter, upright in his saddle and sitting loose.

Little bitty lightweight Harvey with the good ears and the quick grin.

133

The kid was mounted on a range cayuse that wasn't a hell of a lot bigger than him. The pony's short, spindly little legs were going hell-for-fifty, though, and the two of them had come up beside Longarm easy as you please.

"Turn them," Longarm barked at him. "Got to get ahead of the leaders and turn 'em east. Big circle."

"Right, Tom." Harvey veered his pony close beside Longarm's much bigger mount and reached over to snatch the slicker out of Longarm's hand. The kid didn't own one of his own. That was something Longarm hadn't thought to buy for the boys at this late season when the rains should mostly be over with.

The kid grinned, nodded a thank-you, and leaned forward in his saddle.

The ugly little cowpony, with more speed and bottom than any sane person would have thought to expect, put its ears back and dug into the sod, those little hooves churning up a fog.

Harvey pulled away from Longarm, outdistancing him easily and riding toward the stampede leaders.

He pulled even with them and a little ahead.

"Now!" Longarm shouted. "Pinch over on 'em!"

Harvey flapped the slicker, cracking the trailing oilcloth like a whip, and pulled his horse in a shallow arc to the left.

The running cattle shied away from him. It was the beginnings of a turn.

"That's right, Harvey. Again."

Harvey turned his horse tighter into the cattle and brandished the slicker. Longarm, riding the flank behind him, applied pressure on the trailing body of cattle.

He tried to look behind to see if anyone else was working with them, but the boil of dust was too thick for him to see more than a matter of rods to the rear. He and Harvey might have been alone in the world. Or the rest of his crew and all of Joe Holcroft's could be back there hard at work somewhere.

Still, it looked like the leaders were definitely turning now, and the rest of the stupid sons of bitches were following as blindly in the turn as they had in the stampede.

"Keep 'em turning, Harvey!" Longarm shouted. He hoped the kid could hear—thank goodness for those good ears—because the noise of the run was awesome and the distance between Harvey's horse and Longarm's slower one was steadily increasing.

"Turn 'em, kid!"

Harvey snapped the yellow slicker in the air, and the radius of the circle shortened a little more.

Longarm lost contact with the kid in the dust and concentrated on doing what little he could to keep the herd together.

Chapter 14

Longarm reached forward with a groan of protest against the countless aches in his muscles and accepted the refill that Goose offered from the coffee pot. He took a short sip of the hot beverage and swished it around inside his mouth, then spat it out. Even so, he could still feel the grit of dust on his teeth. Tired as he was, he would damn sure welcome a chance to sleep, but as long as the day had been the night likely would be just as long. Once a herd had been heated up by a run they could be hard to control for days afterward. And they would never again be as calm and reliable once they had experienced the terrors of a stampede.

A Holcroft rider named Chance rode into camp and dismounted. "Hey, Tom."

"Yes?"

"I heard they've found your horse string. Leon's bringing them in now."

"Thank goodness for that," Longarm said wearily. At least now he would have a bedroll. Little time to use it, maybe, but he would have it when the time came. "How's your drag man?"

Chance shrugged and helped himself to coffee. The Holcroft crew was not so tired as Longarm and his boys. They had been caught out of position when their drag rider's horse fell with him, and most of the work of containing the stampede had fallen on Harvey and Longarm and the other two boys, who had been riding three-quarters of a mile behind when the stampede broke.

"Joe says he has a broke leg and likely some busted ribs too. But nothing come through the skin so there likely won't be infection. He'll get over it."

"That's good."

"Not much we can do for him in camp, so Joe's sending him back to Stateline. They're s'posed to have a sawbones there."

"Bad break. You boys were short-handed to begin with."

Chance looked to Goose for advice and got a nod of approval. "Me and the rest of the boys," Chance said, "got to thinking about that. An' what we suggested to Joe was that he bring you an your boys into our crowd for the rest of the drive. Your cattle is all mixed in with ours now anyhow. It'd be a waste of time to sort 'em all out. So we thought maybe we could all work along together till we get to the chutes. I figure Joe'll go for it."

"I know I would," Longarm said, "if it means we can get a little sleep soon."

"Your boys did all right," Goose said.

The three of them were not in the camp at the moment. Roy had felt so bad about losing control of the remuda and pack string that he had insisted on going out in the night to look for them, and Willie and Harvey had insisted on going with him.

"You want I should fire a gun three times to signal them

138

kids in?" Goose asked in mock seriousness.

One of the other Holcroft men picked up a clod of dirt and chucked it at him. The clump struck him between the shoulder blades, and Goose laughed.

It had been a damn fool with a sixgun who had started the run earlier. The red-faced cowboy had explained that he'd gotten off his horse to take a crap and was just getting comfortable when a rattlesnake buzzed behind him. Said it sounded like the thing was inches away from his bare backside.

Before he had time to think what he was doing, he had his gun out and shot the snake's head off.

And before he had the time to regret the reaction, the whole damned herd had reversed direction and was intent on leaving this noisy country behind.

If Longarm hadn't been so bushed by the work involved in stopping the run, he probably would have thought the story a funny one. Maybe he would laugh at it tomorrow.

As it was, though, it reminded him of what a gun-ready crowd this Holcroft bunch was. They seemed to be set on a hair trigger all the time. Habit, certainly, but an unlikely one in a trail crew. It was a curious thing.

Still, the Holcroft crew was damn well appreciative of the help Longarm and his boys had given them. If those kids, Harvey in particular, hadn't been behind the Holcroft herd, the beeves would still be running.

"Joe and the rest of our boys will be in soon," Chance said. "They'll make it official, what I told you."

"We appreciate it," Longarm said. "It does get tiresome when there's so few to handle the night shifts."

"With a herd big as ours," Goose said, "we like to keep four men riding all the time. But with your bunch joining up with us we'll still be able to ride nighthawk only a third o' the night instead of half like you've been doing."

"You won't get any argument out of me," Longarm said. "We eat pretty good, too," Goose said with a grin. "All the better once we take the choice meat off all the broke-legged cattle we strung out today."

Longarm got to his feet and stretched. "I better go see if I can find my crew. Gotta tell them the remuda's been found or they'll be out there all night."

"You can borry one of our spare horses if you've a mind to, Tom. Yours looks like it'd fall over sideways an' die if you asked more of it tonight."

"It ain't the only one that feels that way," Longarm said with a grin. "But I'll take you up on that offer."

"Time you get back we oughta have some steaks cooked an' biscuits to sop in the juice."

"Then point me at a fast horse, boys, 'cause I don't want to be late for that."

They were coming closer to Ogallala, but Longarm was coming no closer to a decision about Joe Holcroft.

Even riding right along with his crew, it seemed impossible to sort out whether Holcroft was the snaky son of a bitch Billy Vail thought him to be, or just a man in the cow business who had found an unusual way to turn a profit off someone else's beeves.

Holcroft never said or did anything... exactly... that would point fingers at the man. But there were sure enough odd little things around the evening camps that led to questions.

Like, for instance, the way the crew played cards every night. Nothing particularly unusual about that in itself. Plenty of trail crews liked to pass the short evenings with a deck of cards or a pair of dice or sometimes a three-card monte game going on a blanket.

But these boys did it for sizeable stakes, cartwheel dollars instead of pennies on the blanket. And in cash, too, not promises to pay once they got to Ogallala and collected wages from the drive.

There was apt to be a couple of hundred dollars on the blanket at any one time. The games were damn sure too rich for Longarm's purse, although he was invited to sit in if he wanted.

Another thing that struck him funny was the way his own boys reacted to the Holcroft men.

It wasn't like there were any hard feelings between the two crews. Nothing like that.

But Longarm really would have expected the youngsters to buddy up some to the "real" drovers in the Holcroft crew, especially since several of the Holcroft men were close in age to Willie and Harvey and Roy. More experienced, sure, but that never stopped a bunch of half-crazy youngsters from getting along with one another.

Yet Longarm's boys not only continued to look to him as their one and only boss, they tended to hang tight together and ignore even the young members of Holcroft's crowd.

Ignore would be too hard a word for it, he decided. Not ignore, then, just not get close to—or apparently want to get closer with them.

Daytimes when they were working back in the drag, the customary place for the inexperienced, the three boys stayed together, and any time Longarm turned to signal them he could be sure it was him and not Joe Holcroft they were watching and taking their orders from.

Nights they either hung close to Longarm or kept to themselves, laying their bedrolls out together and just a few feet apart from wherever the Holcroft men were bedded down.

That, too, was a puzzlement.

Still, the boys were able to relax a bit more now that the herds were mixed together. More hands meant lighter work, even with a herd the size of this one, particularly at night, when each man was able to get something close to eight hours of sleep instead of the four or five they had gotten used to since Dodge.

Longarm and his boys were assigned the middle watch

each night, so their sleep was interrupted, but there was more of it and he was grateful for the change.

The food was damn sure better. Leon did nearly all the cooking for the camp, and it turned out the job was his because he was almighty good at it. In fact, he'd have been able to double his usual trail wages if he'd been willing to sign on with some outfit as a full-time cook.

Assuming he drew ordinary trail wages. The level of nighttime betting made Longarm wonder about that.

Yet, damn it, there was really nothing Longarm could put his finger on with an exclamation of "aha!" and say that Billy Vail was right or wrong.

Two days out of Ogallala, Holcroft called him aside after supper and walked out onto the grass with him in the darkness. The cattle were bedded about a quarter of a mile out and were peaceable. There hadn't been a repeat of the stampede, and with every day of quiet that passed it became increasingly unlikely that they would booger again.

"My men have taken a liking to you, Tom," Holcroft said, "and I have to say you and your boys've been a big help to us. We'd have been in a fix if we'd had to come on short-handed."

"It's been a help to us, too, Joe. That extra sleep comes in mighty welcome about the dawn roll-out time."

"Well, I wanted you to know that I appreciate it, Tom. To show that I do, I have a proposition for you." Holcroft smiled and accepted the cheroot Longarm offered him. He paused while they both lit up, then said, "I admit that this isn't an entirely selfless idea, Tom. It would save you and us some work, too."

"Go ahead. I won't make any promises, though, till I hear what you have to say."

"You might have heard how I do my business, Tom. These cattle we're trailing aren't mine. I have them on consignment from owners who brought them up to Dodge. I guarantee each owner a premium of a dollar a head if he allows me to bring his beeves north. And, of course, I'm entitled to whatever profit there is above that."

Longarm nodded.

"The thing is, we still have your herd—what is it, four hundred head or so?—mixed in with ours."

"Three eighty-five," Longarm told him, "less whatever we may have lost in the stampede."

Holcroft waved his hand as if brushing that matter aside. "We won't quibble about a beef or two. Say three eighty-five then."

"So?"

"So if you like, Tom, I can just go ahead and market yours right along with my consignment herd. Give you the same deal as I made with the owners back in Dodge. Pay you off cash on the barrelhead once we get to Ogallala, and then it's my concern to find the best price for them. The current Dodge City price plus a dollar. My good fortune if it turns out more and loss if it comes in less."

"But if it's more," Longarm said, "I'd lose, because my cattle will already be in Ogallala. All I'd have to do is cut them out from yours and sell them myself."

Holcroft shrugged. "All right. Then, to save the work of cutting the herd, I'll agree to pay you the Ogallala price, whatever it is. But you tell me tonight, before either one of us gets a look at the chalkboard over at the depot, which way you want to have it. A dollar over the Dodge price or smack on the Ogallala price. Would that suit you better."

"You're an easy man to get along with, Joe. I got to say that about you."

"Which do you want, then? Or go your own way, of course. It's up to you."

Longarm pretended to think about it, but in fact he did not have to. By opting for the current Ogallala market price he would have more of an excuse to hang close to Holcroft.

"Ogallala current," he said. "And we don't bother cutting the herd."

"Fair enough, Tom." Holcroft extended his hand and the

two men shook on the deal.

"Like I said, Joe, you're an easy man to deal with."

"I'm glad you think so."

"More?"

"This is plenty, thanks." Longarm accepted the tin plate of fried meat and boiled beans and carried it away from the fire to where the boys were sitting cross-legged on the ground in a little group of their own. The Holcroft men were gathered ten or fifteen yards away.

"Hello, Tom." Harvey grinned and moved over a bit to make room for Longarm to join them.

Longarm hunkered down between Harvey and Roy and dug into the food. The cattle were quietly nooning, with only a skeleton crew watching over them while the rest ate.

"Good, huh?"

"Better than your cooking, as I recall."

"Yeah." Harvey grinned again and wiped his greasy fingers on his thigh.

Longarm hid his amusement in a mouthful of steak. The boys were still acting like they were on a holiday. Where most hands will squat to eat or hunker over their spurs, the kids were sitting smack down on the ground. It was like they were reveling in the idea that they could wallow in the dirt all they wanted and no one was going to holler at them about it. They could wipe their hands on their britches and no one cared.

"Company coming," Longarm said, looking out past the grazing herd.

"Time to relieve the watch already? Shit, I ain't done eating yet." Being able to cuss all they wanted seemed also to be a novelty still, although their basic good manners kept them from indulging overmuch.

"No. Looks like a carriage."

"Way the hell out here?"

"Take a look for yourself."

Roy stood and shaded his eyes. "It's a carriage, all

144

right. Coming right down the trail."

Officially, by act of Congress, they were on a road. In actual fact, the only discernible roadbed was where the passage of cattle had beaten the grass down. A few years of disuse and there would be no sign that a road had ever been here, although down on the Santa Fe and up north on the old Oregon Trail the years of iron-tired wheels had cut ruts into rock as well as sod. Those marks would likely remain for generations, even though the Oregon Trail was never formally a road, while this insubstantial Ogallala route was.

The carriage swung wide around the herd and came closer. It was drawn by an unmatched four-up. A man was driving, but there was the unmistakable sight of petticoats and a parasol behind him.

"A woman," Willie said in wonder. "I'll just be go to hell."

"Mind your tongue, Willie," Harvey said.

"Yeah, an' you mind yours." Now that there was a woman in the neighborhood all three boys reverted to civilized ways. Willie and Harvey removed their hats and slicked their hair flat with the palms of their hands. Roy went so far as to get up and brush the dirt off the seat of his trousers. Longarm tried hard not to smile at the preparations they were making. They probably didn't realize themselves what they were doing at the mere sight of a skirt in the distance.

Once clear of the herd of cattle the carriage turned back toward the noon camp. As it came closer Longarm recognized the passenger: Mrs. Joseph Holcroft, Kathleen Holcroft, formerly Kathleen Morehouse of Beaumont, Texas.

Joe Holcroft left his men and hurried to help her down when the carriage stopped. The driver knew enough to keep the rig far enough from the cookfire so dust wouldn't get into the food.

"What a pleasant surprise, dear. I wasn't expecting to see you until tomorrow," Joe said.

"And I wasn't expecting to find you so far south, dear."
Kathleen raised her cheek to him for a kiss. "You are slow
this trip."

"We had a little trouble a few days ago. It slowed us
some." He offered his arm and led her toward the men, all
of whom were standing now with their plates in their
hands, while Marty went to fetch a folding camp chair
from the back of the carriage and set it up for her.

Kathleen glanced toward Longarm and his boys. She
raised an eyebrow, and Holcroft leaned close to whisper an
explanation to her.

Longarm's boys seemed a bit perplexed by the visit, but
the Holcroft crew took it in stride. Apparently it was perfectly normal for Mrs. Holcroft to join them for the last leg
of the journey into Ogallala.

Holcroft beckoned for Longarm and the youngsters to
join him, then made the introductions.

"Yes," Kathleen said. "I recall meeting you in Dodge
City, Mr. Custis."

"Yes, ma'am."

"Joseph tells me you and your men have been a great
help to us this trip. Please accept my thanks as well as his."
Her glance in the direction of the boys was enough to set
Roy Garrett into a red-cheeked flush of pleasure. There
was something about Kathleen Holcroft, and not just her
looks, that could make him feel plumb silly, in fact. Longarm could feel it working on him, too, although it was
directed now at the boys. Willie hemmed and hawed a bit
and then mumbled an aw-shucks sort of thank-you for all
of them.

Kathleen looked pleased with herself. Obviously she
was well aware of the effect she had on men.

"It is a pleasure to meet you all," she said softly. Then
she turned her attention back to her husband. "Joseph,
dear, may I have a word with you, please?"

Longarm and the boys went back to their dinner, while

146

Holcroft and Kathleen wondered off slowly in the direction of the herd.

They were a handsome couple, Longarm thought. Distinguished-looking. Downright genteel and rich-looking, even if Joe had gone belly-up in the cow-raising business down in south Texas.

Longarm saw Joe slide an arm around Kathleen's still slim waist as they wandered and talked after their separation.

He thought about Billy Vail back in Denver.

Chapter 15

Longarm rode left drag. He didn't have to. It was simply the proper thing for him to do as an intruder of sorts on the larger herd, so he volunteered.

And in truth he had an ulterior motive for being back there, very much apart from range courtesy. It gave him an opportunity to keep an eye on Kathleen Holcroft.

Her carriage was trailing the herd and holding to the west of the north-moving column of steers, where the prevailing wind off the distant mountains would keep the dust away from her. It was the boys riding right flank and drag who were having to eat grit with all their meals.

Longarm watched Kathleen surreptitiously, careful not to be obvious about it. The observation had little or nothing to do with the job at hand. He was plain curious about her.

She was an almighty fine-looking woman, silver in her hair or no. As a young woman she would have been a real beauty. Enough to make a grown man slobber at the jaws and bark at the moon. Whatever had been before . . .

He tried not to speculate about that, but it was impossible not to. He wondered if Mrs. Vail—good and gentle person that she was—knew anything about Kathleen.

Hell's bells, Longarm didn't even know if Billy's infatuation with a far younger Kathleen had been back in his bachelor days when he was a wild kid with a badge on his vest and a sixgun on his belt, or if the thing had been later, after Billy was married and trying to settle down, at least to the limited extent that a lawman is ever able to settle into a solid and respectable way of life.

Longarm rejected that line of thought, angry with himself even for raising it. If he knew Billy Vail, Longarm's money had to be on the affair—or whatever—having been before Billy hooked up with his missus.

Still, it must have been a damned powerful experience for him. Something very special.

Not that Billy had ever talked about it. Longarm never would have known a thing about Kathleen Morehouse Holcroft except that Henry tipped him to it.

Quiet, damn near invisible Henry always knew an awful lot more than he cared to say.

Well, Henry had known about this too. How over the years Billy had kept quiet tabs on Mr. and Mrs. Joseph Holcroft of McMullen County, Texas.

And how once each year, just as regular as clockwork, for no apparent reason but always on the same date in June, the distinguished United States marshal for the Denver District went off and got himself stinking, falling-down drunk.

Henry hadn't actually *said* there was any connection between this elegant-looking woman and Billy's annual drunks. But Longarm got the unspoken impression that Henry might have bird-dogged his boss on one or more of those wet June evenings and heard Billy say more than he ought.

And that cool, gracious lady riding right over there in

that carriage was the female who seemed to have tied Billy into knots for all this long time afterward. She sure as hell must be something extra, Longarm thought.

He shook his head. It was one thing to think about that. Hell, everybody had a past of one kind or another.

What was bothering him, though, was whether this assignment came about because Billy Vail thought Joe Holcroft was really up to something wrong on these Dodge-to-Ogallala drives, or if it was really a question of Billy wanting to get some revenge on the man who had finally ended up in Kathleen Morehouse's wedded bed.

That was a bitch of a thing to wonder about, but, damn it, it was Custis Long's job that was on the line here too.

If this turned out to be a vendetta, well, he and Billy and likely Henry as well would be out on their asses and looking for gainful employment.

That bullshit about jurisdiction, for instance, wouldn't hold up if anyone bothered to look too close at it. Federal case, indeed!

The only thing Billy could come up with—and the man was no slouch when it came to making a weasel fit into a wormhole when he was looking for jurisdiction—was that the drives were taking place over a federal-government-owned road right-of-way and therefore should be considered a federal case.

Well, if that twisty little piece of rationalization could be said to hold water, then anything that happened on federal land, including open range that hadn't yet been taken up and patented under one of the homestead or timber or grazing acts . . . well, damn near *anything* would have to be considered a federal crime and investigated by deputy U. S. marshals. Everything right on down to nabbing pickpockets or hoorahing people for killing porcupines—which was actually and honestly against both law and common sense.

The whole thing was a bitch, Longarm thought, and if he hadn't felt so strongly about Billy Vail he would turn right here and ride west toward Denver, and the hell with Joe Holcroft, the borrowed army steers, and all the rest of it.

But he'd accepted the assignment, damn it. He'd started on this job. He would see it through.

What really bothered him, though, was what Billy would feel and do if Longarm came back and told him that Joe Holcroft was a strange damned businessman, but straight arrow as far as the law was concerned.

And that, by Godfrey, was what it was sure looking like at this point.

Neither Joe nor any of his men had actually done a thing that was beyond the law, federal or state.

Longarm took another glance over his shoulder toward Kathleen and reached into his pocket for a cheroot. He was having some longing thoughts about the little bit of Maryland rye that remained in his saddlebags, but that would have to wait until evening camp was made.

For the time being he would just have to content himself with a smoke and shift in the saddle from his left cheek to his right.

He grinned tightly to himself. That was one thing that wasn't bad on this job anyhow. Having to use a big old stock saddle instead of his usual horse-saving McClellan made it a much more comfortable ride. A man could actually slop around and ride easy in this Frazier.

He jammed the cheroot into his jaw and thumbed a match afire. What the hell. He still had a job today.

"Hot damn, Tom, will you lookit that?" Willie was excited, and so were the other boys. At the first sight of Ogallala they began to sit straighter in their saddles and make little gestures toward brushing the dust off their jeans. Not *too* much, though. They were, after all, seasoned trailhands now. They were entitled to look a bit dusty. Hell, they were expected to. They had the *right* to some dust, by jingo.

Longarm smiled at the boys and the way they were taking the thrill of reaching trail's end. As far as he could see, there wasn't all that much about Ogallala that was particularly thrilling.

There was the gleam of late-afternoon sunlight on the rails that justified the town's existence, but other than that it was a pretty dreary scene.

The South Platte River ran by, but that was damn sure no thrill. Flat, shallow, and treacherous, the south Platte was not a river to inspire poets, or be much of anything else but a nuisance.

Basically the thing was the asshole of rivers. A man got used to it being a stream that any self-respecting mule could outflow with a good, healthy piss. Then just about the time said man accepted the South Platte for the miserable thing it was, the dang thing would jump up and go to flooding the flat countryside for miles on either side of it. And it would be plain embarrassing to be drowned by a river that was too shallow for a man to take a bath in for nine years out of ten.

Longarm shook his head and grinned again at the way the boys had commenced to preen themselves for a big night on the town.

"I won't have money to pay you off till the cattle sell," he told them, "but I reckon I can come up with a couple of dollars for each of you." They were pretty damn good kids. "We'll call it a bonus, not an advance." That part—why not?—he could pay out of his own pocket and keep it off the government voucher for expenses. They'd earned it.

"Thanks, Tom."

"Remind me before you head in," he said. He kicked his horse into a lope and circled it back toward the carriage where Holcroft was riding beside his wife for these last few miles.

"Mr. Custis," Kathleen greeted. She gave him a brief flicker of a smile and a cool nod. He thought she looked

153

preoccupied, and perhaps a touch nervous too.

"Ma'am." He took off his beat-up Kossuth and nodded politely.

"You haven't come dunning me for your money already, have you, Tom?" Holcroft asked. The man's voice was jovial and enthused. Unlike his wife, he seemed to be in high spirits indeed. Certainly he seemed unworried about the price of beef he would find posted on the depot boards and the gamble he had taken when he guaranteed the herd's consignors their profit.

"No, Joe. I just wanted to ask if you already have a buyer lined up or will you bargain."

"Oh, I have a man here who I've dealt with on the other herds this year. But I've made no promises to him. We'll hold the herd back under light guard until I do some talking." He smiled. "You never take the first offer, you know. Might be passing up a bonanza that the next fellow'd be wanting to give away."

"You have more experience at this than I do, so I'll take your judgment on it."

"I take that as a compliment, Tom. Thank you." Holcroft reached into an inside coat pocket for a fancy leather cigar case and offered Longarm a pale corona that looked very much like the ones Goose Coe sometimes smoked. Holcroft was practically vibrating with energy and anticipation now. He kept looking forward toward the roofs of Ogallala.

"Thank *you*, Joe." Longarm accepted the cigar and lighted it. The thing was every bit as good as he remembered.

"Tell you what, Tom. If you like, since you do have beeves of your own to sell in this deal, you can come with me when I meet with the buyers."

Kathleen gave her husband a cross look, but he either did not see it or chose to ignore it.

"That's might fine of you, Joe. Thanks."

154

"After supper tonight, then, Tom. We'll be staying at the Rance House. You can meet me there, and we'll go see if we can do some business with these sharpies from Chicago." Holcroft's satisfied expression said that whatever happened, he intended to have it all over the Chicago sharpies tonight.

"I'll be there, " Longarm promised.

Hell, this was better than he'd hoped. Now there could be no question about his being able to discover the details of Joe Holcroft's dealing. Not when Billy Vail asked. And not if the U. S. Attorney asked, either.

For the past couple of days Longarm had found himself having more and more such thoughts about the possibilities of an official inquiry if everything turned out the way it now looked.

At least this way we would be able to give them a full and fair report on the subject.

"See you later, Joe."

"It will be my pleasure, Tom."

Kathleen Holcroft said nothing as Longarm turned his horse away from the carriage.

At least she didn't say anything while Longarm was still within hearing. Taking a guess based on the woman's expression, though, Longarm expected her to have a word or two with her man afterward.

"Stuart Reilly, Lem Johnston, Cal Parker, I want you gentlemen to meet Tom Custis. Tom has cattle thrown in with my herd, so he is interested in our discussion tonight." Holcroft introduced the buyers, all of them gathered at the same table, and motioned for the waiter to bring a bottle and glasses, even though most of a bottle was already on the table before the Chicago men.

Longarm was glad he had dressed in his best for this evening. He still looked somewhat on the shady side because that was the way he had come prepared for the job, but for tonight he had made himself as presentable as possible and had gotten a shave and haircut and bath at the barbershop down the street.

They were gathered in a private room off the Rance House's gentlemen's lounge—which was what the high and mighty called a saloon back East—and the surroundings were downright grand.

"You made a quick return, Joe," the buyer named Johnston said. "What shape are your beeves in?"

Holcroft chuckled. "Do you think I don't know you'll already have looked them over, Lem? Of course you have. It's what I'd do myself. We moved right along and had one run, so they aren't exceptionally fat. But they haven't been gaunted either, Lemuel. Range-run steers, the same quality as I always deliver. Thrifty but sound. And no disease that I'm aware of. They should travel well for you in the cars, with minimum shrinkage."

Johnston nodded. Parker said, "While we were out admiring the herd, Joe, I assume you will have checked the prices posted."

Holcroft nodded.

Joe Holcroft had looked at the board. And so had Longarm, even before he treated himself to the cleaning up.

The current Ogallala market price was a respectable $42.20 per head. Respectable in a declining market, but only seventy cents above the Dodge City price.

Longarm knew damned good and well that Holcroft had guaranteed his consignors a return of $42.50, but Holcroft did not seem at all worried about the difference. If the man was putting on a bluff for the benefit of the Chicago men, he was doing a damned fine job of it.

"I have, Cal, and I must say that I'm disappointed. But you and I both know that my herd will be one of the last to arrive in Ogallala this season. Certainly it will be the last herd of any size that you boys can bid on. And once the shipping season ends, you will be forced to buy at high prices off the eastern farms."

"Yes, but any surplus range steers we take on now will have to be fed at eastern prices until they're needed for slaughter, Joe. We all know that, too," Reilly said.

Holcroft spread his hands. He still looked confident.

"How many head do you offer?" Parker asked.

They were interrupted by the arrival of the waiter with Holcroft's bottle and a tray of clean glasses. The man cleared away the soiled glasses that were already on the table and replaced the ashtray with a clean one also.

For the sake of courtesy the buyers ignored the already opened bottle and cracked Holcroft's to pour drinks all around. The liquor turned out to be bourbon, not to Long-arm's taste, but he was in no position to complain.

"You were about to tell us what we're expected to bid on," Johnston reminded when the drinks had been poured and sampled.

"Including Tom's herd," Holcroft said, reaching into his pocket and producing a small notepad that he flipped open and consulted, "we should have five thousand, four hundred twenty-three head of sound longhorns, gentlemen. Less, of course, any losses en route. The figure is subject to tally entering the yards here." He snapped the book closed. "You'll not have another opportunity like this until next season, gentlemen."

Stuart Reilly peered down into his glass and shifted his weight on the chair. Reilly, Longarm guessed, would not bid on the herd. Not seriously, anyway. Probably the amount would be too large for him to handle.

Longarm tried to calculate just how much money they were talking about on a herd that size.

A hell of a lot, that was for sure.

He would want a pencil and paper to work it out exactly, but five thousand head at just over $42 apiece would be something like...hmmm...5,000 times 40 would be $200,000. Plus whatever the overage was.

That was one *hell* of a bunch of money.

Parker wasn't shy about figuring it out exactly. He

pulled a notepad out and did the calculation. "At current market, Joe, you're looking at $228,850.60."

Of course, the actual amount would matter little to Joe Holcroft. His profit had to come from the amount he could get over and above $42.50. Longarm knew that even if the Chicago men did not.

If Holcroft lost just thirty cents per animal it would be an out-of-pocket loss of something more than $1,500. And that was *before* he paid wages and expenses.

Holcroft reached for the bottle and topped off each man's glass. He really didn't look a lick worried. Longarm reminded himself never to play poker with Joe Holcroft.

"You know I don't expect to sell for current market, boys," he said cheerfully. "You know and I know that this is your last shot at filling your yards for the winter price rise. You'll hold these cattle a few months and sell them for forty-nine or fifty dollars a head. Maybe better, from what I hear about the Midwestern grain crop this year." He smiled. "Those farm boys in Iowa and Illinois have themselves a good crop this year. More than enough grain to carry their farmyard cattle through the winter. So they won't be anxious to dump their dairy beeves at a loss. Not this winter."

Parker frowned and seemed to think about that. Johnston studied his own fingernails. Reilly just tried to look polite. Longarm was convinced that this deal was too rich for whatever packing house Reilly was here to represent.

"I might . . ." Parker said slowly. "I might go another dime with you. Out of friendship and the business we've done before, Joe."

Holcroft chuckled. "Friendship has nothing to do with it, Cal. You need those beeves. But you'll have to pay to get them." His eyes shifted toward Johnston, who pursed his mouth and steepled his fingers before he spoke.

"Well, Lem?"

"Fifteen cents," Johnston said. He sounded reluctant. Longarm guessed that there might be some deductions

158

from Johnston's commission on the deal if he went too far with the bidding.

Parker took a drink, thought for a moment, and nodded. "Twenty cents, Joe. That's as far as I go. If Lem wants to go higher they're his cattle."

Holcroft looked at Johnston. The man hesitated only for a moment. Then he shook his head.

The cattle were Cal Parker's at $42.40 per head.

At that rate, Joe Holcroft stood to lose something like $500 for his efforts, plus whatever he had to pay out to his crew and whatever expenses he had put into the drive. *And* the cost of whatever cattle they might have lost along the way. They wouldn't have a figure on that until the steers were counted into the yard and became Parker's property, because if Holcroft or his men knew about a steer being missing it wouldn't have been lost.

Whatever the final figures turned to to be, though, Joe Holcroft had lost on his gamble this trip up the trail.

Yet even so he appeared relaxed and at ease, even jolly about the whole thing.

No, by damn, Joe Holcroft would not be a man to face across a poker table.

If Longarm hadn't known for absolutely certain-sure that Holcroft was taking a bath on the venture, he would have sworn that the man had just come out fat on the deal.

He was good. By damn, the man was certainly good.

Longarm helped himself to a refill from the Chicago men's bottle. Holcroft had enough money problems right now. Longarm did not want to take anything from him.

Chapter 16

The boys came wandering back to the herd just in time for the middle shift of nighthawk. They'd bathed and gotten haircuts—poor ones, so they likely had saved a little money by chopping on each other's hair—and they smelled of beer and cheap perfume. All that on two dollars apiece. Longarm was impressed. But then he remembered how it was to be young and happy and on the prowl. Good for them.

"Come along, gentlemen. One last tour around the herd."

"Did Mr. Holcroft find a buyer for the cows?"

"He did. We'll deliver them to the pens tomorrow." He glanced toward the stars wheeling slowly overhead and corrected that. "Later today, that is. And we'll get our share of the payoff afterward."

"All *right*." Roy looked anxious to get his hands on some real money. Apparently Longarm's little bonus had only whetted the youngster's appetite.

The boys saddled their night mounts and hobbled the day horses they had been riding before turning them loose for what was left of the night. Longarm was already saddled and ready to go.

"Sure am glad you fellas ain't late," one of the Holcroft men said when Longarm and his crew showed up to relieve the early watch. "We was afraid you wouldn't come."

"Now it's our turn to worry about the morning crowd," Longarm agreed.

The Holcroft riders did not bother to go back to camp. They made a beeline from the herd straight to town. They acted like they had some money in their jeans and were afraid Ogallala was going to shut down before they got a chance to spend it.

Longarm put Willie and Roy in a clockwise rotation around the quiet herd, then sent Harvey off counterclockwise. He hung back for a bit, giving Harvey time to get halfway around the herd before Longarm started his own lullaby walk through the night.

He heard a horse approaching from the direction of the trail up from Kansas and moved toward it, wanting to intercept whoever it was before the rider could unknowingly spook the herd. If there was anything they didn't need at this last minute, it was another stampede.

"Slow up," Longarm called softly. "Got a herd ahead of you."

The rider came closer and Longarm saw that it was the Holcroft man who had been detailed back to Stateline with the injured rider some days back.

"Who's that?" the man demanded. "Oh, yeah, I remember you. You're the one that was tailing us the whole damn way from Dodge."

"That's right. Joined the bunch just after you left. This is Joe's herd we're riding watch on, so move easy, will you?"

"They got in all right, then?"

"No more problems. How's your friend?"

"Dead." The man certainly sounded unconcerned about it. But then he would have had some time to get used to it. It was not news to him.

"From a broken leg?"

The man shrugged and began to roll a cigarette. "Turned out to have got his insides scrambled too. It happens."

It happened, all right. More cowboys died from bad falls and bad horses, probably, than from every other possible cause thrown together. The trails from Texas to Kansas were lined with a string of shallow-dug graves.

"I'm sorry to hear that."

The Holcroft rider shrugged again. He acted like he personally didn't give a damn either way.

"Joe's in town?" he asked.

"At the Rance House."

"All right, thanks." The rider finished building his smoke, lighted it, and drifted away into the night in the direction of Ogallala. Even this late at night it would have been impossible to miss the town. The lights from it were near enough to put a glow in the sky, and Longarm expected the town would be going at full speed until dawn brought a new day of commerce.

"How's it going, Goose?" Longarm hooked his elbows over the stock-pen rail beside Coe.

"Not so bad, Tom, now that these sons of bitches is off our hands. I'm glad to be shut of them, let me tell you. Never liked damn cows. Didn't when I was a kid an' don't now. Smelly, stupid damn things. No account at all unless they're on a plate."

It was an odd sentiment from a cowhand, but the man was entitled to his opinion no matter what he did for a living.

"What will you do now that the droving season is over, Goose?" It was the sort of conversational thing that a man asked. Nothing more than that.

"The crew's splitting up. Won't be any more work for

163

us. I don't know. Maybe drift up Montana way. They say there's plenty of open range up there yet." Goose grinned. "I know. You're likely thinkin' that men like us can't settle down. But I been thinkin' about giving 'er a try. Take up a claim on some water an' buy some stockers. Maybe even buy some patented land up there. I ain't stupid, you know, like cows. I seen the way things are going down south with all the wire coming in. The day'll come when a man has to own his grass or get shut off from it. But I don't know." He thought for a moment, then laughed. "Maybe what I ought to do is buy me a saloon someplace. Change my name and get respectable. How d'you think I'd look in a boiled shirt and necktie, Tom?"

"Like a monkey, same as I would."

"You're prob'ly right. But I don't know. Maybe I really will look around for something respectable to do. You know. Invest my money. Find a decent woman, even." He laughed. "Wouldn't *that* be something. Cigar?" He offered Longarm one of his dime cigars, and Longarm was quick to accept it.

Longarm struck a match and fired up the coronas for both of them. "Been saving up, have you?"

"Naw, I . . ." Coe hesitated and frowned a little. It was like he was remembering something. "Yeah, Tom. I been salting my wages away for quite a spell now. An' now that the outfit's breaking up, well, I might as well put it all to work."

"I don't blame you," Longarm said. "Me, though, I can't ever save enough dimes to build a dollar, one month to the next. But I expect you're steadier than I am." He slapped Goose on the shoulder and turned away from the pens. The last of the Holcroft herd and the few that belonged to the army were being driven inside the gate wings. Longarm's boys were over there on horseback, enjoying the work so much that they'd wanted to stick with it to the last possible moment, which this was. "I'll see you later, Goose."

"Any time, Tom."

"Really. I still owe you that drink. I haven't forgotten."

"I'll hold you to it, too."

Longarm stuffed his hands into his pockets and ambled along toward the gate. He looked perfectly at ease and unconcerned with the world in general.

In fact, he was doing some serious thinking.

Calvin Parker offered his right hand to Joe Holcroft to shake. And with his left hand passed over to the older man a check drawn against a Chicago bank for $229,229.20. The final count into the pens had shown a loss of only fifteen head of cattle on the drive from Dodge city, a figure that was quite good when the stampede was taken into account.

It was, Longarm thought, a hell of a lot of money.

Even his own share—the army's, actually—was an appreciable sum. Longarm had figured it out last night at $16,324. Even that relatively small amount would be enough to set a man up for a long, long time.

The two men concluded their business, with Holcroft signing a bill of sale made over to the packing house, and Holcroft motioned for Longarm to come with him.

"We'll go over to the bank now, Tom. Can't make change out of a check, you know. I'll put this on deposit and have them make you out a check for your share of the sale."

"Cash would be better," Longarm grunted.

"Of course," Holcroft agreed.

They walked together to the Stockmen's Bank of Commerce, and Holcroft held the door for Longarm to enter.

Longarm was tense as he entered the bank. If Holcroft intended to take his profit from Longarm's contribution to the herd—which Longarm had to consider as a possibility in light of what he knew about the man's business dealings and apparent lack of concern—he would either try to disappear now or, more probable, would have Longarm waylaid once the cash from the sale was in his hand.

Holcroft seemed perfectly at ease, though. He bypassed the two tellers' cages at the front of the bank and went directly to a desk at the rear where a youngish man in coat and tie greeted him by name.

"I have everything all ready for you, Mr. Holcroft," the bank officer said.

"Excellent, Harry. This is Mr. Custis. The gentleman I told you about."

"Yes, sir. I have his check all made out." Harry opened a drawer of his desk and removed a check.

"Mr. Custis would prefer cash, Harry." Longarm had not yet had an opportunity to say anything. Holcroft was taking complete charge of the transaction; indeed, he had had everything arranged well in advance.

"That will be no problem, sir." Harry gave Holcroft a broad smile and Longarm a considerably reduced one. Holcroft was, after all, the big supplier of cash flow through the institution, while Longarm was just a rundown-looking newcomer.

Harry found a printed form and began to fill it out. "Would you like to pick up your . . ."

"Later," Holcroft said quickly, even though the bank officer had not yet indicated which of them he was speaking to or what it was he intended to ask.

"As you wish, sir."

Holcroft glanced at his pocket watch and said, "Tomorrow, Harry. I'll come by in the morning."

"Yes, sir." Harry finished filling out the payment slip and handed it to Longarm. "You can present this at the window for your money."

Longarm nodded and left the other two. When he did, Holcroft leaned forward over the bank officer's desk and said something in a voice too low for Longarm to make out.

The money was paid quickly and without an eyebrow being raised, in gold coin, at Longarm's request. Cash transactions were common in the cattle business. A great many of the old-time cowmen trusted no form of paper.

The coins were delivered in a canvas bag that was all too obviously a bank bag. Longarm asked if something else might be available.

Apparently that request, too, was entirely common. The teller transferred the bright coins to a less conspicuous burlap sack and handed them over.

"Joe, it's been a pleasure doing business with you."

"My boys and I are grateful for your help, Tom. I'm almost sorry in a way that you didn't take me up on that offer. You could have made a few dollars more if you'd accepted the Dodge-plus-a-dollar price."

Longarm shrugged. "It was a gamble. Wouldn't be any fun if a man won every time."

"Exactly," Holcroft said with a seemingly genuine smile.

"Thanks again, Joe."

No one followed him when he left the bank, and no one was waiting outside or anywhere nearby to try to take the money from him. He had more than half expected that, but no one in Ogallala seemed to be paying any attention to him at all.

He took a circuitous route through the town, out of sight of the business district, and made a brief stop at a smaller, competing bank a few blocks away.

When he left there, certain he had not been followed or observed, he was still carrying the burlap sack, but now the bag contained nothing more interesting than several pounds of lead slugs.

Even so, no one seemed at all interested in Tom Custis or the bag he was carrying.

So much for that stillborn theory.

And if that was so . . . *why the hell wasn't Joe Holcroft worried about all the money he was losing?*

Chapter 17

Longarm ordered a glass of Maryland rye—a large one, thank you, and stand by for refills—and savored the taste of it with pleasure. His evening carry-along bottle was empty, and the bourbon these cowmen preferred was a poor substitute.

"Hey, Tom, we been looking for you." Willie settled in at the bar next to him with Harvey and Roy Garrett. The boys still looked pleased with themselves after the grand experience of a real trail drive.

"I hadn't forgotten about you," Longarm said. He grinned at them. "You didn't think I'd gone and run out on you, did you?"

"Shee-oot, no, Tom. We know better'n that."

"Buy you a drink?" Longarm motioned for the bartender and ordered, "Whiskey for these young men, if you please. This same good rye as I'm drinking."

Roy grinned and looked so shy that Longarm had to wonder if he'd ever had anything stronger than beer before.

"Sorry to be so late getting your pay to you, fellows. I had a few things I had to do." He reached into a pocket for the gold double eagles he had set aside to pay the boys' wages.

"We looked for you. Didn't have much money left so we made ourselves a supper outa the supplies left over from the drive," Willie said. "I hope you don't mind."

"Of course I don't mind."

Harvey nudged Roy in the ribs. "Ol' horny here wanted to look for you in the whorehouses, too, but they wouldn't let us in without any money."

"Well, you have money now if that's where you want to spend it." He handed each of them their pay and said, "The saddles and bridles are yours to keep. The blankets and oilcloths, too, for whatever that's worth. The horses, when you're done with them, you can turn in at the livery. I'll take care of them when I get around to it. No hurry about that, though, if you need transportation for the next day or so."

The boys looked like a bunch of canary-eating felines. Longarm could tell that they figured the whole wide world was right out there in front of them and they, by damn, had it by the tail.

"You wanta come do some high spending with us, boss?"

"That's just about the nicest offer I've had in a long while, Willie, but I'll have to pass. There's some more business I have to take care of tonight. Got a few people to see and some wires to send. But I thank you. Would you mind a piece of advice?"

"No, sir. O' course not."

"Then find a place to leave those shooters that I see you've strapped on again now that we're away from the herd. Guns and good times sometimes don't set well together."

"Aw, we wouldn't get in no trouble, Tom."

"Not us," Harvey put in.

"If you say so," Longarm said.

"You can trust us."

"I can for a fact," Longarm agreed.

The boys downed their whiskeys, Roy taking his like medicine instead of the excellent rye it was, and left the saloon with their spirits high.

Longarm had a good idea of where they were going, and very likely the girls of Ogallala would be able to teach them a few things that young hands just couldn't learn on a dusty trail drive. He wished them well.

Hell, he might even have gone with them—and it really had been nice of them to ask him along—except that he had things to take care of before the night was over.

Longarm shaved and dressed with care. For the first time in weeks he was aware of the way he looked. He missed the comfortable familiarity of his usual clothes. In particular he missed the old brown Stetson when he dragged the floppy, dirty Kossuth onto his head. He wanted to look and feel normal today, a matter of pride in himself and in what he did. Still, his everyday clothing was back in Denver and he was in Nebraska, and that was that.

He did, though, slide the Colt in and out of its holster a few times to make sure it was free in the leather and took more than the usual care with the set of the holster and belt for a draw that could be made from habit rather than conscious—and therefore slow—thought.

He left the hotel room and tipped his hat to a late-working girl who was just leaving a room across the hall. She wasn't all that bad. Some blemishes and bruises showed under the powder on her face, in itself out of place in the daytime, but all in all she wasn't bad.

She gave him a professional smile and a wink as they passed, but he returned only a shrug and a thin smile of apology. There were other things that needed doing this morning.

Instead of eating at the hotel, he walked down the street

171

to a cafe he had seen in the same block as the Stockmen's Bank of Commerce. It looked reasonably clean.

It was early, well before normal business hours, but the cafe was crowded. Longarm waited patiently until he could get a table near the front window. He ordered a hearty breakfast. "And coffee. I'll be waiting for a friend, and it may take a while, so keep the refills coming."

The food was good, the coffee not particularly so, but that was all right. He could stand it. And he was patient.

At 8:26 by the reliable Ingersol, Joe Holcroft and Marty showed up at the end of the block.

Promptly at 8:30 the shade covering the front glass at the bank was raised and the door was unlocked. Holcroft and Marty were the first customers through the door for the day's business.

Longarm reached into his pocket for a silver dollar and dropped it onto the table. His bill would be far short of that, but he did not want to take the time to wait for change.

"Another refill, sir?" The waiter had to repeat the question twice before Longarm heard.

And even when he answered, refusing the offer, he did not take his eyes from the door across the street.

Holcroft stepped inside the shed behind the livery. He almost ran into Marty, who had stopped just in front of him, and he had to take a moment, blinking, while his eyes adjusted to the deep shade.

The kid who was running the livery was nowhere around. Not that he would have suspected anything anyway. He struck Joe as being the kind of straight, dumb asshole who would assume the best about people. No suspicions, no brains. The hell with him.

The men who were gathered inside the shed began to ask questions, but Joe waved them to silence.

They had no way of knowing it, but he considered them very nearly as dumb as that kid in the barn. Followers, every one of them.

172

"Is everyone here?" Joe asked in a commanding voice.

"Everybody but Goose. Last I seen him he was throwing his guts up in the crapper behind Maybelle's place."

Someone sniggered, but Holcroft's stern expression cut that short. "This is it then," Joe said. "What we've all been working for this whole summer long."

He reached into the leather folio he was carrying and pulled out a packet of paper.

Paper that was inked green on one side, gold on the other. Paper currency, redeemable anywhere in the country for real gold. Hundred-dollar bills, stacked and wrapped in sheaves of fifty. Five thousand dollars each, and one packet for each man in the crew.

Five thousand dollars was a princely sum for any of these broken-down gunslicks. Ten years' wages for a working stiff. No wonder they had been so willing to go along with him on the deal.

Holcroft's lips twisted in silent amusement. Apparently it had never occurred to any of these sheep that the distribution would still leave him and Kathleen with more than $150,000.

But then, that was the difference between a sheep and a wolf. Sheep never thought. It was the wolf that was entitled to the winner's share.

Casually Holcroft tossed the first packet to Marty, then one to Leon, and on around the eager, snickering circle.

"Five thousand apiece, boys. Just like we planned."

"Mighty glad we hung with ya, Joe," one of them mumbled. The man was actually trembling as he held the sheaf of bills in his grimy hand. Even knowing the nature of these pathetic men, Holcroft could hardly believe that.

They were greedy. He had known that all along. But they were so *petty* in their greed. That was what truly amazed him. They risked so much for so very little.

Not that it mattered now.

The long summer of heat and dust and smelly cattle was over now.

All the losses on those early small herds had been paid

173

out of pocket. Holcroft did not resent that expenditure at all. He had been dealing with more sheep when he took on those consignments and met those guarantees. He had been more than willing to pay the cowmen their supposed profits out of his own small savings.

After all, that was what had allowed him to set the suckers up for this end-of-summer score.

It had all been worth it.

Kathleen was a brilliant woman. The plan had worked every bit as well as she had said it would.

Now the two of them could retire to Boston. That was where Kathleen really belonged anyway, not on some hardscrabble ranch, no matter how big or seemingly elegant. Kathleen had taught him a great deal.

And now the reward for all their troubles was at hand.

Best of all, Joe Holcroft would never again have to deal with sheep like those cattle consignors or like his own working crew.

Never. He had sworn that to himself within minutes after Kathleen outlined her plan for their salvation.

No wonder he had failed down in Texas. He and Kathleen were meant for better things.

Now and for the rest of their days they would be able to live the life they truly deserved.

Joe felt good as he distributed the last of the money packets. Good. Even munificent. Stronger and better than he had felt in years.

"I won't be seeing any of you again," Joe told his men. "We have been together a long time, and you have served me well. Now we must part." He dropped his voice half an octave to give the words of parting an air of solemnity and sorrow. The truth was that he was damned well enjoying this speech. He thought he sounded rather fine.

"My advice to you, men, is to change your names. Move on. Prosper. I would give you a recommendation, but..." He paused to chuckle aloud. "Within a week or two, when those consignors fail to receive their funds, I suspect that my recommendation would be worth little to you.

"Still, men, I wish you well. Each of you. I shall never forget you." That much was the truth, anyway. He would not forget them. Malleable sheep they had been, but useful ones. In a manner of speaking he was grateful to them.

"Goodbye—" he went on.

"Joe."

"What?" Holcroft snapped. Everything had been going so nicely and now Marty had to go and ruin it all with a question.

"I was wondering. You know. About Goose's share. D'you want me to take it for him? I could see that he gets it."

"Oh." Holcroft had forgotten about that. He was not a petty man. He would not have dreamed of jeopardizing the venture by shorting one of the crew. Not, at least, until he was safely on the train east and well away from them. "Yes." He gave Marty the last packet of bills. The rest of the money was securely placed in a draft against a Chicago bank in a fresh and untainted name. That detail had been one of his own contributions to the plan, taken from his experiences in trying to sell cattle as an owner himself. Drafts, after all, were much more secure than cash. Only a fool would trust his fellow man enough to carry immense quantities of cash with him on a long trip across the nation. "Thank you, Marty."

"Now, men, I must—"

Shouts and the loud intrusion of running footsteps sounded just outside the shed door.

"Open up!" a voice called. "This is the sheriff. You're surrounded. Leave your guns and come out with your hands raised."

Marty and most of the others were already clawing for their revolvers.

Joe Holcroft felt faint.

Chapter 18

Whatever the signal was, Longarm missed it. With no warning whatsoever, the area was suddenly full of running, shouting men with guns in their hands.

A bunch of them poured out of the livery barn. More came running from an alley behind the livery. A group of cowboys who had been examining the feet of a heavy draft horse in the corral near the shed suddenly grabbed for their revolvers and joined the rush.

All of the men had revolvers. A good many of them had shotguns or rifles as well.

The man who seemed to be in charge of the assault stopped in plain sight right in front of the shed door and cupped his hands in front of his mouth.

"Open up! This is the sheriff! You're surrounded. Leave your guns and come out with your hands raised."

Longarm stepped out of the alley where he had been waiting.

There was a moment of silence that was quickly shattered by a roar of gunfire from inside the shed.

The sheriff died in that first volley of fire. Longarm saw him start to buckle forward from a slug in the stomach, then even more quickly jerk upright again as another bullet hit him flush in the forehead. He dropped like a hog in a slaughterhouse.

"Oh, shit," Longarm muttered to himself.

The deputies outside—if that was what they were—returned the fire, so many guns going off so quickly that it sounded like a roll of thunder.

Wood splinters and puffs of dust flew from the walls of the shed as the flimsy building was riddled with hot lead.

Someone screamed inside.

Leon and the man called Chance appeared in the shadowed doorway. Leon's left arm was broken, blood running off his fingertips. He braced himself against the doorframe, Chance beside him. The two men now became the primary targets for the eager and angry deputies.

Chance went down in a firestorm of lead. Leon remained where he was, ignoring the bullets that ripped at him. He raised his revolver, took careful aim, and shot the nearest deputy in the chest.

The deputy fell to his knees, blood spewing from his mouth, and Leon reeled backward into the shed as yet another swarm of slugs tore him apart.

With two of their own dead, the deputies redoubled their fire, carbines and shotguns booming, revolvers contributing their sharper, lighter reports. The combined roar was enough to drown out a steam whistle.

Longarm darted forward. He grabbed the biggest deputy he could find and spun the man around to face him.

"What the fuck is going on here?" Longarm demanded.

The deputy's eyes got wide when he saw the big Colt Longarm had in his fist. The man went pale.

Longarm snatched out his wallet, carefully hidden away until this morning, and flipped it open to expose his badge. "I asked you what the fuck is going on here."

The deputy gulped once, then leaned forward to take a close look at Longarm's identification. Only then did he relax. The other locals were still pouring fire into the livery shed. If it kept up much longer the whole damn building was likely to be cut apart and fall down onto whatever was left of the men inside.

"We got . . . it's an arrest, damn it. A lawful arrest."

"Arrest? It looks more like a slaughter. And not a one-sided one either." Longarm had to raise his voice to make himself heard.

At least one of the Holcroft men was still alive and returning the gunfire. Another deputy, a young, clerkish-looking fellow who belonged in a storeroom, not a gun-fight, screeched and grabbed his leg. His trousers were smeared with bright red. He turned and hopped for cover on his one good leg.

"Who are you supposed to be arresting? And why?" Longarm persisted.

"Just a minute. Now that the sheriff's dead you ought to talk with the chief deputy, Marshal." The local pulled away from Longarm, paused to snap a cylinder of .44-40s into the shed, and ran to a group of men who were crouched behind a wagon. Longarm could see the local man talking to a slender, red-headed fellow with a badge pinned promi-nently on his vest. The redhead nodded and dashed across the livery yard to where Longarm was leaning against the side of the barn, out of sight from the shed.

"I'm Johnny Borland," he said. "Merle's chief deputy." Merle, Longarm guessed, would be the dead sheriff. "Tim said you're a federal marshal?"

"Deputy marshal," Longarm said, "Denver District. What's going on here?"

"We got a tip early this morning that a bunch of cow thieves were supposed to meet in that shed this morning to divvy up the loot from a big steal. So Merle got this posse together, and we came to make the arrest. You saw what happened afterward, I reckon."

"You say you got a tip?"

"That's right. A note. It was slid under the jail door sometime during the night."

Longarm was doing some fast and furious thinking.

The gunfire was beginning to subside now. The deputies were firing much less rapidly, and no return fire could be heard from the shed now.

In all probability, Holcroft and everyone of his men were dead by now. Any who were still alive would be damn sure shot up.

No one could have escaped all that unscathed.

"The handwriting on that note," Longarm asked, "it wouldn't have been a woman's, would it?"

"How'd you guess that?" Johnny Borland asked.

"Lucky."

"Yeah," Borland admitted. "The way Merle figured it, some whore overheard something and didn't want to get herself involved with the law. You know. Something like that."

"Uh-huh," Longarm said.

Without another word to Borland, who probably would be considered the acting sheriff now that Merle was dead, Longarm turned and began to race down the street.

Behind him he could hear Borland shouting, "Ease off, boys. Slack off, now. I need a volunteer to go see what we got in there. You. With the shotgun. Come over here."

Son of a bitch, Longarm thought as he ran.

The Colt was still in his hand, forgotten for the moment in his urgency.

The desk clerk balked at Longarm's request only until he saw the blued-steel Colt. Then it became perfectly acceptable policy for the hotel to give out the room number of a lady guest.

Longarm took the stairs three at a time, made a wrong turn in the corridor upstairs, and had to double back, checking the room numbers as he went.

He was in a hurry. If he was guessing correctly, and if

he was remembering the railroad schedule correctly, he was cutting it close. He might already be too late.

He reached No. 19 and listened outside the door. Someone was in there, all right. He felt a surge of relief. Not too late after all. He relaxed and waited. There were footsteps approaching the door.

The knob turned, the door swung open, and Kathleen Holcroft stood facing him. She had a handbag looped over her wrist and a small bag in the other hand. Behind her he could see luggage packed, closed and stacked on the bed, awaiting the bellman.

"Good. I was afraid you would be late, and—" She stopped in mid-sentence as she recognized him.

"Mr. Custis." She smiled, making the adjustment quickly. "I am sorry, but Joseph has already left this morning. Business. Now, if you would excuse me . . . ?"

"I don't think so, Kathleen. Fact is, I think you're inexcusable." He pulled out his wallet and showed her the badge.

"I work for Billy Vail," he said. "You remember him, I'm sure. He sent me. Do you know why? He wanted to *protect* you. He thought Joe was up to something no good *and he wanted to protect you.*" Longarm did not know that, not exactly, but he believed it. It had to be the truth of the matter. Billy had sent him out on this one thinking to protect Kathleen Morehouse Holcroft.

Even Billy Vail could make damnfool mistakes sometimes.

Kathleen did not wait to ask questions or make excuses, and it took her no time at all to decide what to do.

She dropped the bag she had been carrying and swung her handbag in a snake-quick arc toward Longarm's head.

He ducked, taking the blow on the shoulder. Whatever she was carrying in there was damned heavy.

Kathleen slipped past him into the hallway and ran for the stairs.

Longarm grabbed for her as she went by but came away

181

holding the shawl that had been draped over her shoulders. He started after her.

Long skirts, awkward shoes, handbag and all, the damned woman could run like a white-tail doe. She hit the stairs three jumps ahead of Longarm and started down them.

"Goose, thank God it's you. Help me. He's after me."

Until then Longarm had not noticed that Goose Coe was standing at the foot of the stairs. Goose must not have been in the shed with the others. He had a gun in his hand.

"Shot him, Goose. For God's sake, shoot him!" Kathleen screamed.

She stopped on the landing and turned, her hand dipping into her purse and coming out with a little nickel-plated revolver.

"Help me, Goose! Shoot him!"

She raised the gun toward Longarm, but he was concentrating on Coe, watching the man's eyes.

It was Kathleen who was ready to shoot.

He didn't want to shoot a woman, damn it.

But she was sure as hell fixing to put a little bitty bullet into Longarm's gut if she could manage it.

Coe fired first.

Longarm's attention had strayed to Kathleen for only an instant, but that had been more than enough time for Goose to complete his draw and get his shot off.

Longarm did not believe he had ever known a man who was faster.

Certainly none who was faster than Goose Coe was that day, if only because of the hatred that fueled his speed.

Coe's bullet slammed into the small of Kathleen Holcroft's back and drove her sprawling forward onto the stairs.

"No!" Longarm shouted.

He was too late.

From the lobby door behind Coe three more guns spat, filling the hotel lobby with the stink of burnt powder.

182

Goose went down at the foot of the stairs, his cheek coming to rest in a growing pool of Kathleen's blood.

Longarm shoved his Colt back into the holster and went down, past Kathleen's body. He was sure she was dead but he took the time to kick her revolver off the staircase anyway. And on down to Goose.

"I'm sorry, Goose."

Coe was still alive, but barely.

"I know, Tom. I wouldn't've shot you."

"Of course not. Hell, man, I still owe you that drink."

Longarm was smiling at Coe when the man died.

"It's all right now," Longarm said to the boys.

All three of them were there, guns still in their hands, but forgotten now in the enormity of what they had just done. Harvey and Willie were pale and looked like they might be sick. Oddly enough it was quiet, shy Roy who seemed to be taking it the best.

"It's all right, fellas. You were backing me, and I appreciate it. How'd you get in on this?"

It was Roy who felt up to answering. "We heard all that commotion down at the livery. And we seen you running down the street with your gun out. Figured there was bad trouble some kind. Then we seen Goose run after you with his gun out. So we knew it was trouble. So we came along behind. He was gonna shoot you, and . . . Wasn't he? Wasn't he gonna shoot you, Tom?"

"Yes," Longarm lied. "You boys saved my bacon."

He gently pulled Goose's eyes closed, then stood.

Goose hadn't been gunning for any lawman. Loyal, dependable Goose had also figured out what must have happened to Holcroft and the crew. It was the turncoat Kathleen he was here gunning for.

But, Lord help them, there was no way Longarm wanted any of these boys ever to know that. They were feeling bad enough from their first gunfight. He sure as hell didn't want them to know that they shouldn't have fired.

183

He looked down at the dead bodies on the hotel stairs and thought about the many more that were down at the livery.

There was going to be an awful lot of explaining and form-filling after this one.

Just to verify his suppositions, Longarm picked up Kathleen's handbag and opened it. As he had expected there was a bank draft there, made out to Mr. and Mrs. Anthony J. Rolfe, exactly as the bank president had told him last night that Holcroft ordered. The bank president had assumed the draft was a consignor's payment. Longarm had known better. The packets of cash, of course, would have been to pay off Goose and the other boys.

Longarm shook his head.

"Are you all right, Tom?"

"Yeah, thanks." That was another thing that was going to need explaining, that he wasn't Tom Custis after all. It was going to be hard to do.

The boys had been loyal enough to Tom Custis that they were willing to kill a man to back him up and never ask what for or whether the boss was in the right.

It was going to be hard now to explain to them that he wasn't Tom Custis.

He hoped they would forgive him for the deception. Maybe if he told them gently enough, and in just the right way, with all the explanations it took.

Longarm squeezed his eyes closed and felt overwhelmed by regret almost to the point of grief.

Explaining things to Willie and Harvey and Roy wasn't going to be anything compared with what would have to come after.

The truly hard thing would be trying to explain all this to Billy Vail.

He looked at Kathleen's body on the stairs and for a moment he was almost sorry that it had been Goose who had killed her instead of him.

Not that that would have solved anything, of course.

It wouldn't have gotten Billy told about the woman a young Ranger had once loved. He must have loved her deeply to care so much still after the passage of so many years.

"Let's go down to the saloon, boys. I have a lot to do today, but first I want to have a drink with you and do some explaining. Would you mind?"

"Mind? No, we wouldn't mind, Tom."

Longarm put an arm over Roy's broad shoulders and another over Harvey's. He motioned for Willie to come along and led the three of them out of the hotel and down the street.

"I hope you'll give me a chance to explain all this," he was saying. "I hope you'll hear me all the way through before you decide what you want to think. But the truth is . . ."

Watch for

LONGARM AND THE DESERT SPIRITS

ninety-ninth novel in the bold
LONGARM series from Jove

coming in March!

The hottest trio in Western history is riding your way in these giant

adventures!

The Old West will never be the same again!!!